ROYAL DOC'S SECRET HEIR

AMY RUTTAN

Recycling programs
for this product may
not exist in your area.

ISBN-13: 978-1-335-64176-2

Royal Doc's Secret Heir

First North American Publication 2019

Copyright © 2019 by Amy Ruttan

Printed in U.S.A.

Books by Amy Ruttan

Harlequin Medical Romance

Hot Greek Docs
A Date with Dr. Moustakas

Christmas in Manhattan
Navy Doc on Her Christmas List

Royal Spring Babies
His Pregnant Royal Bride

Hot Latin Docs
Alejandro's Sexy Secret

Tempting Nashville's Celebrity Doc
Unwrapped by the Duke
Convenient Marriage, Surprise Twins
The Surgeon King's Secret Baby
A Mommy for His Daughter
NY Doc Under the Northern Lights
Carrying the Surgeon's Baby
The Surgeon's Convenient Husband

Visit the Author Profile page
at Harlequin.com for more titles.

For my prince charming who swept me off my feet twenty years ago when we first met and who continues to do so.

CHAPTER ONE

IT HAD BEEN a long time since she'd been home. Jeena's heart beat triple time as the relief plane that was carrying medical supplies and her team of doctors and nurses approached the island kingdom of Kalyana.

She took a deep calming breath as the cloud cover evaporated and the jewel of an island set against the Indian Ocean came into view.

Her home.

Only Kalyana hadn't been her home. Not for a long time. Not since that night ten years ago when her father had woken her up and told her they were leaving Kalyana.

They were *all* leaving because they were in danger.

She hadn't wanted to go and didn't know where they were going, but her parents needed her and she needed them. So she'd left Kalyana for Canada.

She hadn't regretted it. It had been for the best. Still, she'd never thought she'd see Kalyana again.

She glanced down at her Canadian passport gripped tightly in her hand and *hoped* she'd be allowed in.

Her father had made it clear they couldn't go back. They should never go back. They hadn't been banished, but her father had said they weren't welcome in Kalyana. Because of her indiscretion, they would be judged. Harshly.

Jeena still found that hard to believe in this day in age, but her father had been adamant. He wanted to protect her and her unborn child.

The Canadian consulate had assured her that the visa had been cleared. That there shouldn't be any issues.

There shouldn't be a risk of someone waiting to pounce on her to ask her about her son and pry into her private life. She knew deep down there was nothing to fear. She hadn't done anything wrong.

All she'd done was become pregnant and decide to have her child. A lot of women were single mothers so there was no reason she would have to watch her back, but still those old anxieties were creeping into the back of her mind. The night her father had insisted they leave. He'd been so scared. He'd thought they were in danger and Jeena knew that someone had made him think that.

And it was all because of who her son's father was. If it had been someone else, they probably wouldn't have left...

"Why do we have to leave?" she asked.

"Lady Meleena said that the King will take your child!" her father said. "We have to go to keep our family together. Your child would be looked down upon. Do you really want that?"

"No." She shook her head. "But we can't afford to leave."

"Lady Meleena will help us. She just asks that we never come back. That we never contact anyone and keep your pregnancy secret. I promised her that for your safety."

"How does Lady Meleena know?" Jeena asked, confused. "No one but Mother and you know. Did you tell someone?"

"Of course not!" her father exclaimed. "Someone at the clinic told her."

"Why would someone at the clinic tell her?"

"Because people know about who you were seen with and it wasn't long before Lady Meleena put two and two together. Meleena's father invests in my plantation. There would be scandal for all of us, and Lady Meleena wanted to take care of us."

"I'm pregnant. I didn't commit a crime!"

Her father hugged her. "Of course you didn't, but Lady Meleena knows first-hand how an illegitimate child with a parent in the aristocracy can be treated. Look at her half-brother Kamal. He was treated so poorly by his peers and then he died in that terrible accident."

"But—"

"No buts!" her father snapped. "We're leaving. It's the best thing for you and the baby. It will protect our family's name and avert scandal for all concerned."

Guilt coursed through her. "Yes, Father. You're right."

Jeena shook the memory away and clenched her Canadian passport tighter in her fist.

The consulate might say that she was cleared to return and work in Kalyana, but was Lady Meleena, soon-to-be royal bride, okay with it?

They'd left ten years ago to save face and her father was indebted to Lady Meleena for her assistance, but then three years ago Lady Meleena had become engaged to the father of Jeena's unborn baby and a little part of Jeena couldn't help but wonder if Meleena had had her eyes set on a certain prize right from the start.

It had bothered her for years that Lady Meleena had taken such an interest in her.

Does it matter? He wouldn't have married you anyway. He couldn't. His family would have chosen his bride, and they wouldn't have chosen a farmer's daughter.

Her stomach twisted and she tried to relax on the last little bit of the long trip from Canada to Kalyana, only she knew she wouldn't feel at ease until they landed and she was cleared by customs. She was breaking her father's promise to Lady Meleena about never returning.

You didn't promise.

Jeena relaxed then. She was different now. She wasn't such a pushover.

This had been her home, whether Lady Meleena liked it or not. She was going to do her job here. She had no wish to interfere in Meleena or Maazin's life.

Even then, she wasn't sure she could relax, visa or not. She glanced out the window again and a lump formed in her throat, tears stinging her eyes as she saw the island get closer.

Home.

This was where her family had lived and thrived on the same vanilla plantation for generations and it was all her fault that it no longer belonged to her family. All because she'd got involved with and fallen in love with the wrong person.

"You okay?"

Jeena glanced at Teresa, one of the other doctors who had come to help with the relief efforts.

"Yeah, fine." Jeena forced herself to smile brightly. "Just missing my son."

Which wasn't a complete lie. She did miss her son. She'd never really been apart from him for this long and with this much of a distance between them.

He was safe in Canada with her parents. His competitive junior hockey team was in the finals and they were playing at Scotiabank Saddledome, which was a huge deal. He'd gone on and on about it for months. As had her father.

Syman was the reason her parents had taken Lady Meleena's aid and come to Canada, and why she needed them. She couldn't have raised him alone in Kalyana or Canada. She couldn't have become a surgeon without their help, and becoming a surgeon had been hard even with their help.

Still, there were things Syman would never know about Kalyana. Things she'd experienced that he'd never get to, like playing on the sand of a pearl-pink beach or swimming in a turquoise sea. Running through her father's vanilla fields or climbing a palm tree to stare out over the Indian Ocean.

Canada had been a good home for them and Syman loved his life there, even with the ice and snow that Jeena had never gotten used to. That she didn't miss.

If you'd stayed in Kalyana, Syman wouldn't even be interested in hockey.

Kalyana was near the Seychelles and was very traditional. Hockey wasn't one of the sports played in Kalyana. If she had raised Syman here, he would probably be into cricket.

Or polo?

Jeena shook that thought away. She didn't want to think about Syman's father and how she had met him during a divot stomp at a match she should've never been at. She had only gone because her friend had dragged her along and during the divot stomp she'd lost her footing and been rescued by the man of her dreams.

Well, she hadn't been completely sure when she'd first met him. Maazin had been a known playboy and she'd known she should keep away, but when he had been with her, he hadn't been the bad boy that everyone had said he was. He had been different.

So kind and caring.

And the more time they'd spent together, the more she'd truly believed he'd loved her.

Her heart skipped a beat just thinking about him. She'd been a fool. Young and naive.

Don't think about him.

Only it was hard not to. He was never really far from her thoughts. The older Syman got, the more he looked like his father, the more she saw the only man she had ever loved. Syman was all the good parts of his father. He was kind and caring. Also driven and stubborn.

Her heart may have been broken, but she

loved Syman and she was grateful that her time with Maazin had given her her son.

"You'll see Syman soon. And I'm sure his team will win the tourney," Teresa said brightly, interrupting her thoughts of Syman's father.

Jeena chuckled. "They'd better or he'll be lamenting it until next hockey season."

Teresa laughed and went back to her book.

Jeena glanced at the reading material she'd brought for the long flight from Dubai, which was just one of the flights she'd been on since they departed from Vancouver. She really didn't know which way was up and given that there was a significant time zone difference, she couldn't help but wonder if Syman had actually won his tournament. Maybe he'd already played?

I should be there.

Only this was her job and her father had taught her and given her a work ethic she stood by. Kalyana needed her and her new country, Canada, needed her to represent them in the best possible light. She understood the customs. She knew the terrain and the people.

Even if it meant facing something that she wasn't sure that she was ready to face.

And when she closed her eyes she could still feel Maazin's arms around her, but then she was reminded of the pain when he'd turned his back on her, when Lady Meleena had told her he'd chosen his duty over her. When Lady Meleena had told her father that Syman would be an outcast. That Jeena would be an outcast because he would not marry her, even though he knew she was pregnant.

Then, a few years later, it had been announced that Prince Maazin had chosen his bride. None other than Jeena's supposed savior, Lady Meleena.

She shouldn't care, but it made her angry. Jeena knew her family had been manipulated.

Don't worry about it. Maazin isn't part of your life.

And she had to keep remembering that.

He hadn't been there for her when she'd had Syman. Neither had he been there when she'd scrimped and saved, worked odd jobs while attending medical school. That had been all her. She didn't need him. She was better off without him.

Syman was better off without him.

Are you sure?

"We're making our final descent into Huban. Please buckle up. It's a bit windy and there has been some damage to the airstrip from the cyclone so it might be a rough landing," the pilot said over the speaker.

"Here we go," Teresa said, setting down her book and buckling up her seatbelt.

Jeena nodded and pulled her seatbelt tighter. She kept her eyes focused on Kalyana as it got closer and closer. She could see the damage. Trees ripped from their roots, buildings along the coast destroyed, but there on the main terminal still flew the blue, green and gold flag of Kalyana. Untouched and fluttering in the strong winds in a clear blue sky. A sight she'd thought she'd never see again.

It helped tame the erratic beat of her heart.

She was home.

Maazin waited on the edge of the tarmac in a van to help transport medical supplies to the makeshift hospital that he and Farhan had set up between Huban and the southeast district, which had been the hardest hit when Cyclone Blandine had ripped through Kalyana.

Kavan, the bodyguard who also acted as chauffer-pilot, had seemed keen to accompany Maazin, but he'd eventually agreed it was best he stay with Farhan, Maazin's older brother, Sara, and her grandfather, Mr. Raj. Ever since the cyclone had hit, Farhan had been jumpy, fussing and fuming over his new bride.

Not that Maazin could blame him.

If he had someone he loved...

Maybe if he still had the one woman he'd once loved he would've felt the same way that Farhan did, but he didn't have anyone.

He didn't deserve anyone. Not even the arranged marriage his father had set up three years ago. Not that he'd really cared for Lady Meleena. It had just been expected and since Maazin had lost the only woman he'd loved when she'd left in the middle of the night, he had settled for the bride his father had chosen. Or eventually settled. After everything that had happened when Jeena had left, he'd spent some time doing what good he could.

He'd served in the Royal Guard and earned his doctorate as a surgeon in the guard. It gave his life meaning, after all his past actions had caused so much pain. His service was the least he could do.

Which was why he'd agreed to marry Meleena. His father had guilted him into it and he had been tired of the nagging to find a wife. He'd had no interest in Meleena, so had had very little to do with her.

Of course, Meleena hadn't liked it too much when he'd devoted his life to healing others, to serving his country, and had ignored her. She'd left him, but no one knew about that yet and that's the way his father wanted it. There were diplomatic policies and contracts at play and his father wanted to wait until it could be properly addressed after Kalyana recovered from the devastation of Blandine.

So he had no one.

No one to worry about. No one to care.

Which was what he deserved.

It was best that he handle this. He was just as capable a doctor as Farhan and Sara were. This was what he lived for. This was all that had mattered since Jeena had left and his brother Ali had died trying to help him. The last thing he wanted to do was put Farhan or Sara in danger.

His mother had already suffered enough because of him. He wasn't going to put Farhan in harm's way when he had military training and could manage this kind of disaster situation with ease. Not that they were in much danger now. The cyclone was over. It was just a matter of picking up the pieces.

Cyclone Blandine had done severe damage to the islands.

He couldn't remember such a storm ever hitting Kalyana.

His father King Uttam was all for Maazin helping with relief efforts. He should be a part of it. Farhan was an excellent doctor, but he didn't have the training Maazin had.

However, his mother Queen Aruna was a little more reluctant to hear a prince of Kalyana was out there helping with relief efforts and getting his hands dirty. She thought it was unsafe.

Of course, even if she didn't show it, Maazin worried his mother had never been happy with anything he'd done since Ali had died.

But Maazin wanted to help.

He *needed* to help.

Still, his mother had made her reservations clear...

"You're a prince!"

"So? What else should a trained surgeon be doing, Mother?"

"You're only a surgeon because of your time in the Royal Guard."

"So what would you have me do?" Maazin asked.

"You should stay in the safety of the palace."

"And tend to royalty? To aristocrats?"

"Perhaps. And perhaps if you had done more of your royal duties and spent time with your betrothed, Lady Meleena wouldn't have left!"

"I don't care that she left, Mother. I don't love her. I couldn't stand be around her."

"Ali did his duty!"

"I'm sorry that I'm not Ali."

His mother's had a faraway look as she murmured, "You're right. You're not..."

Maazin winced. He hadn't wanted an arranged marriage. Especially with someone his father had chosen only for the betterment of the country.

Your father chose for Ali and he'd been happy. Your father chose for Farhan and he's happy with Sara.

He ignored that niggling little thought.

Right now Kalyana needed him. When Ali had been alive, he'd always been out there lending a hand, and that was the least Maazin could do since he was responsible for Ali's death.

You're not.

Only he felt he was. And he was sure his mother felt that he was responsible for Ali's death. Ever since then his mother had been cold and distant. With him especially.

And he hated it that he was the cause of her grief, that he was just a living reminder of her pain. And he couldn't help but wonder if she wished it was him who'd died instead of Ali.

He pushed that thought aside and watched as the Canadian plane landed with much-needed supplies. Cyclone Blandine had done so much damage and they hadn't been very prepared. Storms had come and gone, but there had never been a cyclone like this. It had formed out of nowhere and so quickly and it had struck so hard.

There was no way they could prepare for quite how extreme it was and they were lucky that it hadn't done even more damage.

The plane from Canada that he'd been waiting for made its landing. Maazin had made sure that the airport runway in Huban had been cleared of debris so that they could receive assistance from other countries, like Canada, and he had his sister-in-law Sara to thank for that assistance.

The plane circled as the winds were high.

Maazin waited with bated breath as the plane came around again then touched down. He didn't know why he was so nervous about this plane landing, but something about this was eating away at him.

He hadn't felt like this in so long.

The last time he'd felt like this…well, he didn't want to think about her.

This was not the time to think about it. It was not time to think about Jeena. Of course, she was never far from his mind. He was always thinking of her, whether he liked it or not. Always wondering why she'd left him. It drove him mad.

"They're ready for us, Your Highness," his driver, Kariff, said.

Maazin nodded. "Let's go and fill this van with supplies and their doctors. The southeast region is in dire need of supplies and medical help."

Kariff nodded and drove the van toward the large plane that had dropped its rear door to make a ramp, ready to start unloading its precious cargo of medical supplies and doctors to aid them.

Kariff parked close and Maazin got out of the van. He opened the side doors and the back so that Kariff and a couple of the other men he'd brought with him could start loading up.

"Who should we be reporting to?" a female voice asked, which sent a shiver of recollection down his spine. He knew that voice. He knew it well because it was burned into every single neuron in his brain. Just the mere sound of her voice fired them off, bringing every bitter-sweet memory to the surface.

Maazin turned around and came face to face with someone he'd never thought he would see again.

His blood froze and everything around him stopped. He couldn't quite believe his eyes and he wondered if he was dreaming. It was like she had walked right out of his dreams, like nothing had changed, like time had stood still. She hadn't changed one bit. Her rich, dark brown hair was tied back in a braid, just like the first day he'd met her. Her skin was still a warm, rich tawny color.

Her deep brown eyes widened and her red lips, lips he remembered so well the taste of, dropped open for a moment and a subtle pop of coral colored her cheeks. She was just as shocked as he was.

Jeena.

In an instant he remembered when he'd first seen her. She'd looked so out of place and uncomfortable on the polo pitch.

She'd worn a long emerald dress and high

heels as she'd teetered on the grass, trying to flip over a divot.

He'd been so entranced by her and had wondered who she was...

"You'll fall over, trying to flip those divots in those heels."

She looked up, embarrassed. "Pardon?"

Maazin knelt down and took her foot in his hands. "May I?"

She pursed her lips and nodded. He removed her shoe and pried off the large chunk of turf that had been impaled on the end of her stiletto heel. He replaced the shoe and then stood, steadying her in his arms, catching a scent of her perfume.

Jasmine and vanilla. It was intoxicating and he was instantly drawn to her.

"Thank you... Your Highness."

"Ah, so you know who I am."

"Everyone knows who you are," she whispered, and wouldn't look at him.

"Well, I am at a loss. I don't know who you are. I have never seen you at one of these events before."

She smiled. "My name is Jeena. I am here with my friend as her guest."

"And who is your friend?"

"Aishraya Raj." Jeena nodded in the direction of her friend. "Her husband is a dip-

lomat, but I've known Aishraya for a long time."

Maazin smiled and bowed at the waist. "Well, allow me to welcome you to our little match..."

Maazin tried to calm the pulse that was now thundering in his ears. She had been the only one to truly *see* him.

The world thought he was this playboy and he let everyone believe that. The tabloids, his parents all believed it and it had got him off the hook of so many responsibilities, but Jeena had seen past that.

He had been so in love with her. He'd wanted to marry her, even though he had always been afraid and not interested in marriage because he'd felt it would tie him down, just like his royal duty.

And he hadn't wanted to drag Jeena into a life of protocol.

She had been free. Which was why he'd wanted her.

Jeena had left him. Left him without a word, and it was because of her leaving that he'd gone to that party to drown his sorrows and then called his brother Ali to get him.

And that had cost Ali his life, because after she'd left, Maazin had decided to take the bad boy road everyone thought he traveled. Ali came to sweep his indiscretions under the rug and died trying to cover up his mistakes.

It had destroyed him when Jeena had left. It was his own fault, though, because he knew he'd driven her away. He didn't deserve her and he certainly didn't deserve anything now. He knew that.

"Maa... Your Highness." And she curtseyed.

He was angry that she had almost addressed him with familiarity, like he wanted, but had then changed it to a formal address and curtseyed in deference to his station, which he hated.

Were they such strangers?

Yes. They were now. She'd left. He'd never left Kalyana. He'd never left in the dead of night, not telling anyone where he was going. And when he'd tried to find her there'd been no trace of her. It was as if her whole life in Kalyana had been erased.

She'd cost him so much.

You were the selfish one. She cost you nothing.

"I'm surprised that you've returned to the

country you abandoned with such ease," he snapped.

Her expression hardened. "My apologies, Your Highness. I'm the lead surgeon on this relief mission. I'm representing Canada and I'm here to deliver your supplies and lend my services to *your* country." She turned on her heel and walked away.

She was a doctor?

Maazin was shocked, but as she stormed away he couldn't help but smile to himself. She still had that spirit he'd admired in her.

That fire.

That had been hidden under the surface, something she'd tried so hard to control, but he'd known what a strong woman had been under that demure exterior.

It's what he'd loved so much about her then.

Now, to see her standing her ground, it surprised him, but pleasantly so.

It woke up a piece of him he'd thought was long gone and as he watched her walk away, giving out orders, he knew that working with her would be a challenge.

One he hadn't expected.

CHAPTER TWO

JEENA DIDN'T KNOW what she had been expecting. She knew one thing, she hadn't planned on seeing him. Actually, she hadn't expected to see him at all. What was a prince of Kalyana doing at the airport, collecting medical supplies?

Not your concern.

And she had to keep telling herself that. She was stronger now. She could handle seeing Maazin.

Can you?

She'd changed, but had she really expected a bad boy rebel prince to have changed in the last ten years?

No. Well, maybe? One could hope. Other than his engagement to Lady Meleena, Maazin hadn't really been in the papers. Perhaps he had changed? She'd always wondered if that image he'd projected before she'd met him had been an act. She knew one thing was for sure, his appearance hadn't changed at all.

It was like time hadn't even touched him at all.

When she'd seen him there, she couldn't believe her eyes. It was like all those years ago when he had knelt down in front of her on the polo field and stopped her from embarrassing herself in front of a social class that she had not been comfortable being around at all.

His ebony hair was shorter than it had been. Gone were the long curls that had framed his face when they'd first met and he was now clean shaven. He'd lost the neatly trimmed beard she'd loved so much. His skin was deep, lustrous gold and warmed by the heat and sun from Kalyana. And he'd lost some of that baby fat that came with youth, but those green-gray eyes were still the same as they'd bored deep into hers, totally riveting her to the spot.

Making her quiver with desire. Even after all these years apart her body still reacted to him. She remembered the feeling of those strong hands on her, the taste of his lips as he'd brushed kisses lightly on hers.

How safe he'd made her feel when his arms had been wrapped around her.

He turned his back on you and Syman, remember...?

"He knows," *Meleena said in a scathing tone.*

"He knows?" *Jeena asked, stunned.*

"Yes."

"How do you know that he knows?"

Meleena rolled her eyes. "My father is very close to the royal family. That's how I know. Prince Maazin can't commit to you."

"I don't believe that."

Meleena fished out a check and held it out to her. "Here. Compensation for your... situation."

It was like a slap in the face and her heart clenched as she stared at it.

This was all she was worth?

The fact he knew about her pregnancy and had turned his back on her made her firm her resolve. She wouldn't be duped again by anyone.

She was no longer that foolish innocent who could be swept off her feet by a dashing Prince Charming.

He hadn't been there when her family

had sold off everything to start a new life in Canada.

Neither had he been there when Syman was born.

Syman, who had those same eyes as his father.

Syman.

Her heart sank. He always was curious about his father and as he got older she knew it was something she would not be able to keep from him. Not when he could go online and look Maazin up.

He'd learn his father was a prince and a playboy. How his father had turned his back on her. His father's whole private romantic life had been splashed across tabloids around the world. The only romance not there and not known was hers. Lady Meleena's parents had paid people off to keep that secret.

"Dr. Harrak!"

She turned and saw Maazin coming toward her and her heart skipped a beat again.

Stand firm.

She crossed her arms and narrowed her resolve. How many people had tried to push her around when she'd been a resident and learning to become a surgeon because she was short at only five feet four? Too many and Jeena had had to rise above all of that and make sure that her voice had been heard above the others in a competitive medical program.

And on top of all of that she'd raised Syman.

She was stronger than some spoiled and pampered prince who was coddled by parents who gave him everything and ruled a country.

She could handle him. She wasn't going to let a prince sweep her off her feet again. She didn't need saving or a knight in shining armor.

And she wasn't going to be sent back to Canada because he and his fiancée were uncomfortable with her presence in Kalyana.

"I have every right to be here," she snapped when Maazin caught up with her.

"What?" he asked, frowning.

"I have a visa and clearance from the consulate to represent Canada and assist in this humanitarian and relief aid effort. Kalyana may not be my home any longer..."

"I'm aware of that," he answered stiffly. "What I came over to say was sorry. I'm sorry for embarrassing you like that."

Jeena was shocked, but she didn't let him know that. That was different. The Maazin she remembered had been a bit arrogant with people he'd felt deserved it, but he had always been kind and gentle to her. She'd often wondered why he hadn't shown that side of himself to the public.

Of course he'd turned his back on her. She wasn't going to be fooled again.

It had been a painful lesson to learn that she didn't need a prince to come and save her and that she was more than capable of saving herself.

"No apology needed, Your Highness. I forgot myself for a moment, you are absolutely right, I left Kalyana for another country, because it was right for me. Now I'm here on behalf of Canada. I'm home now and I'm here to help." She curtseyed again.

"Jeena, stop that." He was annoyed. She remembered how much he hated protocol. She knew she was getting to him.

Good.

"Stop what, Your Highness?"

"Curtseying and calling me Your Highness. Jeena, we know each other intimately."

"That's Dr. Harrak to you, Your Highness." She crossed her arms and leaned forward. "Perhaps we knew each other once, but a lot has changed. I prefer the formality, Your Highness."

His eyes narrowed. "Fine."

She nodded and felt a bit of satisfaction knowing that she had won that battle. It felt good.

Did it?

"Well, Dr. Harrak," he said, exaggerating her name. "My driver Kariff and I are to take you to the southeastern region, which was hardest hit by the cyclone. Our doctors have been working non-stop since the cyclone hit four days ago and they could use a break."

Jeena smiled. "Of course, Your Highness."

He stood there. "Well?"

"Well, what?" she asked.

"We have to leave."

"I'm waiting for you to lead the way, Your Highness. It's only proper."

He rolled his eyes and turned around and started marching stiffly toward the van, the tail of his blue kurta billowing out behind him.

If she really wanted to bite back at him, now would be the time to tell him that he reminded her of his father, which had always used to annoy him as well.

She chuckled softly and kept that to herself.

Right now, there were patients waiting for help and that was all that mattered to her, but it was nice to have a little victory over the man who'd broken her heart.

A man who had ruined her for all others.

A man who still had a piece of her heart, whether she liked it or not.

The ride in the van was uncomfortable and tense. Maazin sat in the front next to Kariff while she and her team were crammed in beside medical equipment and gear. There would be another van coming soon to take the rest of the supplies and gear into Huban, but right now they were transporting what was most needed to the hardest hit region. That had been her plan. Get to work, help out and keep out of sight.

She might not really care about her father's promise to Lady Meleena but she didn't want the drama that would come with it.

The press didn't know about Syman or her romance with Maazin and she preferred it that way.

The only reason she was here was to save lives.

As the van navigated the damaged streets of Huban, Jeena's heart sank to see the destruction. The little wooden shacks of the poorest hadn't fared as well as the colonial buildings that had been built by the British over a century ago.

There were downed power lines, crumbled stone and debris everywhere.

"Hold on," Maazin said over his shoulder. "This part of Huban was flooded quite badly. The water has receded enough to allow passage, but it will be a bumpy ride."

Jeena bit her lip. Her head began to spin and her pulse thundered in her ears. A panic attack was coming on and she needed to center herself. She needed to gain control, but it was hard. She didn't like water too much. She was fine if she was on a large boat or had her feet firmly planted on the ground, but in a van going over a washed-out road, this she didn't like.

And she closed her eyes and tried to not think about that time when she had been a young girl and she'd wandered too far from her parents' home and down to the small creek that ran adjacent to the plantation.

She'd been playing in the water when it

had begun to rain, but since there had been no lightning and it had been so hot and dry, Jeena had just stayed where she was and enjoyed not being hot for once.

It was then that a flash flood had ripped down the mountainside. She would have been swept away if she hadn't gripped that low-growing palm. She'd held onto the trunk of that tree for what had felt like an eternity as the water had rushed past her, trying to snatch her away and wash her out to sea.

And she remembered the terror of it all.

The water that had rushed over her while she'd clung to life, while she'd tried to breathe and not take water into her lungs. The weariness of trying to stay afloat had begun to set in.

And then she remembered the strong arms of her father reaching down to pluck her from the swollen creek and into the safety of his arms.

She'd gotten into trouble, but not too much as her father had felt that she'd learned her lesson about doing dangerous things and not listening to them, but really she hadn't learned her lesson. Not really.

And how had she repaid her parents?

She'd become involved with a prince of Kalyana, even though it was forbidden because he'd been destined to marry someone of his father's choosing.

Her parents had got her out of the country to protect her. Lady Meleena had helped before'd she got engaged to Maazin a few years later. Her parents had lost everything.

They love Syman, though.

Still, she should've learned to curb her reckless ways that day she'd almost drowned and maybe then her parents would still be in Kalyana and she could've been here with the cyclone had hit and she could've been helping right from the start.

But you wouldn't have Syman.

No. She wouldn't have had Syman and for that she couldn't regret her past mistakes. Even though she regretted everything about failing in love with a prince, there had been one bright spot to the whole thing and that was her son. And that thought made her feel guilty for wishing her mistakes away.

He was her world and she missed him. Especially at this moment when she could do with a smile and a hug. She really missed her son.

The van rocked, jolting thoughts of Syman out of her head. She gripped her seat as the van made its way through another washed-out section of the road. The rushing water caused the van to sway, but it wasn't deep.

It was deep enough for Jeena's pulse to thunder even more loudly in her ears and for beads of sweat to break across her brow. Her hands felt clammy as she dug her fingers into the upholstery of the seat.

She looked up and saw that Maazin was watching her in the rearview mirror. He looked concerned and she tried to shake it all off. The last thing she wanted was for Maazin to feel bad for her.

Or, worse, think that she couldn't handle this, because she could.

Jeena looked away and the van carefully made its way through the water and back onto dry road as they made their way out of the capital city of Huban. Jeena took a deep breath of relief and glanced out of the window. She could see the palace rising in the distance. It had sustained some damage, but it still stood there, like a rock, reminding all the people of Kalyana that the country was still strong.

And a blowhard loud-mouthed king ruling them.

Well, not really. King Uttam might not

be her favorite person in the world, but he wasn't a terrible king. He was a fair ruler.

And she saw a lot of his stubbornness in Syman. When Syman set his mind to something, there was no convincing him otherwise. It made her laugh from time to time. At least Syman was strong.

He had a strong personality. One she hadn't had until she'd had him and had worked her way through medical school.

"We're nearly at the hospital," Maazin announced.

Jeena didn't respond. She just looked out the window toward the Indian Ocean, remembering precious days gone by and how it was all her fault that her son couldn't enjoy this with her.

Maazin watched Jeena as she and her team had a quick meeting and then started to move around the makeshift hospital that was set up in an old shanty town, or what was left of a shanty town now that it had been leveled.

Something had bothered Jeena in the van when they'd crossed through that water and he couldn't help but wonder what.

It's not your concern.

And it wasn't. She wasn't his and could never be his.

Still, he was drawn to her and he was worried that something had happened to her and he felt responsible.

"You all right?"

Maazin turned to see Farhan standing beside him. Farhan looked exhausted and Maazin couldn't blame him. He and Sara had been working hard to help since the storm had started. Farhan hadn't been here when Maazin and Jeena had had their torrid and short love affair.

So there was no need to explain it all now.

It was over.

And it wasn't Farhan's business.

It was Maazin's pain to bear.

"Nothing, just…" Maazin scrubbed a hand across his face. "Tired and relieved that help is here."

Farhan nodded. "So am I. Sara has been working herself to the bone and she needs her rest."

"Take her back to Huban and get rest. I'm going to stay and help the Canadians and help Kariff unload the medical supplies."

"You should rest too," Farhan suggested.

"You've been working non-stop since even before the cyclone hit."

"What for? I have no wife and I like to keep busy."

"You're going to work yourself into an early grave, brother." Farhan turned and left and Maazin let out a breath that he hadn't even known that he was holding.

He glanced back over his shoulder to see Jeena sitting next to a patient's bed and talking with the elderly woman, who seemed to recognize her.

Why had Jeena left?

"She's left," his mother said with finality.

"What?" Maazin asked, stunned.

"Your paramour. She is gone. Now you can do the duty we all must, and marry someone of the lineage to be your bride."

"I don't believe you," Maazin said hotly. *"Jeena would never do that."*

His mother walked calmly over to her desk and pulled out a letter, handing it to him. It looked like Jeena's handwriting.

His mother held it out to him between two fingers. "Read it."

Maazin snatched the letter from his mother and quickly read the letter. It didn't sound like Jeena, but it was her writing.

"Where did you get this?"

"Meleena found it."

"Why would Meleena find it?" he asked.

"Her father has invested in the Harrak plantation and she's trying to prevent a scandal for a family her father supports."

Maazin read the letter again and couldn't believe it.

It stated that she was leaving him because she couldn't stand being linked to a prince who had a checkered past full of women and gambling. Even though she knew those things weren't true...even though he had never been unfaithful to her. He'd wanted to marry her.

Maazin crumpled up the paper. "She would never leave her parents. I'm going to find her."

He turned to leave but his mother cleared his throat and Maazin turned back.

"Her parents are gone too. They left Kalyana with her. This morning, in fact. They should already be in Dubai."

"Where are they going?"

His mother shrugged. "Who knows? They didn't tell me. Kalyanese people are free to come and go out of their country as they please."

Maazin had gone to her parents' vanilla plantation, which was on the westerly side of the main island. And his mother had been right. They had left and their plantation had been for sale. It had made no sense.

And he'd felt betrayed.

So he couldn't help but wonder why they'd left and why she was now back. She'd fled in the middle of the night like she'd been afraid. So why had she come back?

At least now he knew where she had gone and what she had done with her life these past ten years. She'd become a surgeon!

He hadn't expected that.

Why not? You became one too.

"You okay?"

Maazin turned around to see Jeena standing next to him.

"Perfectly," he said.

She cocked an eyebrow. "You sure?"

"Yes," he snapped, and then he sighed. "Sorry. I'm tired. It's been non-stop since we set up this hospital."

"I can see," she said gently, and then tilted her head to the side. "I thought the Royal Guard set up this hospital?"

"They did. I'm part of the Royal Guard."

Her mouth dropped open and then

snapped shut. "You're a member of the guard? Since when?"

He wanted to tell her since she'd left and he'd had that drunken night, the night his brother Ali and his wife Chandni had died.

After the funeral he'd joined the guard to give back and try to appease the pain and guilt he'd felt for surviving when they hadn't.

And when he'd served his first year he'd decided to become a surgeon, to save even more lives.

It won't bring Ali back.

He cleared his throat. "I've been a member of the Royal Guard for almost ten years."

"That seems so unlike you."

His spine stiffened and he wanted to ask her who she thought he was. He hadn't been the one to leave. He'd stayed and made the most of the heartache she'd caused.

"Help!"

Maazin spun around as a man came in carrying a lifeless boy. He ran toward the man, who looked exhausted and sick. He scooped the boy up in his arms.

"Your Highness, please...my son."

"What's wrong?" Jeena asked, coming up beside Maazin and looking at the boy.

"He's burning up," Maazin stated, touching the boy's face.

"He started complaining of abdominal pain two days ago and there was blood..." The boy's father looked pale.

Maazin's stomach dropped and he felt sure he knew what it was.

The boy's father was probably a farmer who got water from the river. After the cyclone the water source had probably become contaminated.

"We need to isolate the boy and his father. I think it's dysentery," Maazin said to Jeena under his breath so as not to alarm the others in the hospital.

Jeena nodded and Maazin took the boy to the back of the hospital. There was a small building that they had the use of with a few rooms for cases such as this. Jeena led the boy's father to one of the rooms as well.

They had to get the two of them away from the other patients as bacillary dysentery was highly contagious, and since Maazin had picked the boy up without gloves he was going to have to go on a course of antibiotics as well and burn his clothes.

At least Jeena had on a surgical gown and gloves, as well as a mask. She was prepared and Maazin had been too busy thinking about the past and letting Jeena's presence unnerve him, so that he hadn't thought about dysentery being a problem after a cyclone. He hadn't changed into scrubs. He hadn't set up to deal with such a contagious disease, and he was kicking himself for not doing it sooner.

He was a fool, but right now he was going to try and save this young boy's life.

The boy winced and moaned in pain, but had a high fever and was completely out of it. Maazin set him on a bed and then got about setting up an IV with a bolus of fluids, electrolytes and antibiotics.

Jeena got the boy's father into the room beside him and through the small window that separated these two rooms he could see that she was doing the same and instructing a nurse, who had put on a hazmat suit, how to set up the quarantine.

Jeena then slipped out of the room and came to him. She looked at the boy and Maazin thought he saw a pained expression on her face.

"You're going to need to get out of those clothes and go on antibiotics in the other room."

"I know," Maazin said. "And you'll have to as well."

She nodded. "I know. I've changed and disposed of the gown, gloves and mask. I'll have the decontamination shower just to be sure, and then get the course of antibiotics."

"I want to make sure my patient's fever comes down." Maazin glanced down at the boy. So small and so sick. He hated seeing his people suffer.

"Your patient? I didn't realize you were a doctor." And he could hear the surprise in her voice.

"Yes. I'm a surgeon, a surgeon in the Royal Guard. My brother Farhan and I have been working here since the cyclone hit. I do my duty to my people!"

"Wow, I'm surprised," she said.

"What? That I'm a doctor or that I'm competent?" he snapped.

Jeena's cheeks flushed in embarrassment. "I'm sorry."

"Thank you," he said. He appreciated her apology.

"Either way, you need to take precautions. Princes are susceptible to dysentery too."

"I'm not leaving my patient!"

"I can take care of that, Your Highness."

A Canadian doctor he was not familiar with came into the room in a hazmat suit. "I think you best go and clean up so we can keep the infection from spreading."

Maazin sighed. "Fine. You're right."

He followed Jeena to where the showers were. She slipped into one of the stalls and Maazin made his way to the other stall. As he passed by, he glanced down at her phone, which was buzzing, and was shocked to see a picture of a little boy on her phone. At first glance it reminded him of his late brother, but there were no pictures of Ali in a hockey jersey. And then it hit him.

The picture was of a little boy with gray-green eyes like his, looking back at him.

And suddenly he felt a bit dizzy.

CHAPTER THREE

JEENA WATCHED THE bolus of antibiotics dripping down and into her arm. It was unlikely that she had dysentery, but given the extremely infectious nature of it, she didn't want to take any chances.

People who weren't treated died.

And it was a painful way to die.

Maazin was in the bed next to her, he was wearing scrubs instead of the kurta that he'd greeted her in and he looked angry as he was hooked up to an antibiotic drip. He was brooding. This seemed to be more like the Maazin she remembered.

Of course she couldn't blame him. She'd be annoyed too if someone questioned her like she'd questioned him.

It just took her completely by surprise that he had served in the royal guard and become a surgeon too. He had never really talked about what he wanted to do because there was no expectation for him to do anything. He was a prince.

And she was impressed that he'd done something with his life.

I wonder what Lady Meleena thinks of his work?

Jeena was annoyed that she let that thought slip in and she was angry at herself for questioning him. She'd apologized, but she knew he was still angry with her.

"We should find out if anyone else is in that farmer's home," Jeena said. "They'll all have to be treated."

"It's just the man and his son. I'm told the boy's mother died last year in a farming accident," he said.

"Oh, I'm sorry to hear that."

Maazin wouldn't look at her. The bolus of antibiotics was apparently far more interesting.

Of course, she couldn't really blame him. Their first meeting a couple of hours ago hadn't been the warmest.

She sighed and closed her eyes, trying to make the best of a tense situation.

"Who is that boy?" he finally asked, breaking the silence.

Her stomach twisted in a knot. "What boy? The farmer's boy?"

He turned and looked at her and then she knew. She glanced down at her phone on the bed beside her. She'd noticed that she'd missed a call from Syman when she'd gone into the shower and she was also very aware that when Syman called his picture showed up on her phone.

And she was also aware of Syman's striking resemblance to certain members of the Kalyanese Royal Family, but she was annoyed that he was asking her who he was.

Had he expected her to use that money to get rid of her pregnancy?

If he had and wanted the money back, she could pay him. The money was still sitting in an account. She hadn't spent a dime of his pity check.

"Who is the boy?" he asked again, his voice calm, but there was a hint of anger in there and that sent a shiver of dread through her.

"My son," she stated. "Obviously."

"Your son? How old is he?"

"Nine. Again obvious."

Maazin's eyes narrowed and then he looked away. There was no sense in hiding the fact that Syman was his. She guessed by his expression, his tone and the fact that Syman was nine that he knew. And there was really no denying it. Syman had the same dark, long curls as Maazin had once had and the same stunning eyes.

He didn't say anything else to her, but she wasn't surprised as the nurses returned to check on them, which was good because emotionally, right now, Jeena didn't want to talk about it. She was afraid if she did she was going to break down and cry.

That was when her phone rang and Syman's face popped back up on the screen. Maazin's gaze locked on that picture.

Not now.

She had to answer it.

"Hi, Syman," she said, answering the phone and feeling Maazin's gaze boring into the back of her skull.

"Hi, Mom!" Syman's voice came from the other end. "We won!"

"You won. That's wonderful."

"Yeah, I'm so excited to get to play at the Saddledome. Grandpa said he's going to take me out for pizza."

"That's wonderful."

"You okay, Mom? You sound a bit weird."

"I'm okay. I'm here in Kalyana and you can tell your grandparents I'm okay."

"Actually, Grandpa wants to talk to you."

"No—" she began, but it was too late as Syman handed the phone over to her father.

"Jeena, are you okay?" her father asked.

She could hear the worry in her father's voice. She remembered how troubled he'd been when he'd found out she was carrying Maazin's baby. Her father had been so terrified Syman would be taken away or that they'd become outcasts.

"I'm okay, Dad. I'm fine."

"You're sure?"

"Yes. I'm working now, though." What she wanted to tell him was that Maazin was here and that he knew about Syman, but now was not the time.

"How bad is the damage?" her father asked. "Have you seen…? How much have you seen?"

Her father was asking about their plantation and whether she'd seen it. Even though her parents had left to protect her and even though her father insisted he didn't care for his old plantation, she knew he did. She knew her father missed his home country.

"I'm outside Huban, in the southeastern

district that was hit the worst. I really have to go, but I'll talk to you later, okay?"

"Okay, Jeena. Be safe and avoid… Be safe."

"I will, Dad."

Her father had trailed off. She knew he'd been going to say avoid Lady Meleena and Maazin, but he hadn't.

Jeena ended the call. She felt like she was going to throw up. This was not how she'd planned this trip to go. All she wanted was to do her job and then head back to Alberta to be with Syman and her parents.

She wanted to lie low.

The last thing she'd wanted to do was run into Maazin but, of course, karma had had other plans. The nurses finished with Maazin and they were left alone again. He wouldn't look at her. He just stared ahead.

"Is he mine?" he finally asked, breaking the silence that had fallen between them again.

"What do you mean, is he yours? Of course he is." She swallowed the lump in her throat, one that had formed because of the tears she'd been holding back for so long. He acted like he didn't know about Syman.

Maybe he'd forgotten and that wouldn't surprise her.

She and her unborn baby had been so insignificant to him, why would he give them a second thought?

"How can I be certain?"

"He's nine years old and you were my first." Jeena wanted to tell him that he was her only lover. That his betrayal of her, his abandonment when she'd needed him most had broken her so completely that she didn't trust anyone else with her heart.

And she had her son to look after. There was no time for romance. All she had was school, Syman and her parents.

The people who mattered most.

"Why didn't you tell me that I had a son?" Maazin asked.

Jeena snickered. "Really?"

"What do you mean, really? You obviously didn't want me to know or you would've told me."

Jeena rolled her eyes. How could she have been in love with someone so stubborn was beyond her. "Don't be so precious. You knew. You've just forgotten."

He opened his mouth to say more but the nurses came back and they removed her IV as she had finished her dose of antibiotics. After she was cleared to go, she slipped off the cot and left the isolation area. She wouldn't be allowed to work on patients until she'd been clear for twenty-four hours and she was annoyed about that, but it came with the territory in emergency medicine. She walked out of the medical tent and made her way down to the beach.

The heat of the sun felt good on her skin. It was way better than the bitter cold Canadian winter that her mother still hadn't gotten used to.

She sat down on the beach and closed her eyes, drinking in the Vitamin D and listening to the sound of the waves lapping gently on the pearl-pink sand. Her mind drifted back to the last time she'd sat on a pearl-pink sand beach like this.

"Jeena, you are so beautiful," Maazin *whispered against her ear.*

A shiver of delight traveled down her spine and she couldn't quite believe that he'd taken her out on his yacht to Patang Island for a private dinner.

There were no guards here.

It was just the two of them on the sandbar,

under the moonlight, with the ocean wind caressing their skin.

She knew that he had a bit of a reputation, but he hadn't been unfaithful to her. They'd been inseparable and she was so in love with him.

He kissed her again, cupping her face and making her melt into his arms. She was so in love with him that she couldn't remember a moment of what life had been like without him.

Life had been so dull and colorless until she'd met him.

"Be with me tonight," he whispered.

She nodded, and he scooped her up in his arms and took her to the private bower he'd built on the sandbar. Their own private retreat, where they were alone, with just the light from the moon reflecting on the ocean accompanying them...

"Jeena."

She opened her eyes and shook the erotic memory from her mind.

She knew it was Maazin.

"I know you have a lot of questions, but since I can no longer work on patients for the next twenty-four hours I have to figure

out a way back to where we're being billeted
and try to get some sleep."

What she really wanted to tell him was
that she didn't have to time to play these
games.

"I can take you there. I have my Jeep
around back and maybe then we can have
a meal together and we can talk about this
in private."

She stood up. "Of course, because you
wouldn't want a scandal."

"No. It's not that. It's for your protection
and for his. Besides, we're the only two potentially exposed to the dysentery. We can't
afford others to be exposed. We need all the
help in the hospitals tending to the injured."

He was right.

And she felt silly. He was trying to offer
her an olive branch and she was being
cranky. She was better than this.

"Fine. I'd appreciate a ride."

Maazin nodded. "My car is over this
way."

She followed behind. She knew it was
for the best they talk this through, but she
didn't want to. What was in the past was in
the past.

Or at least she thought it was.

* * *

Maazin wasn't going to take her to the hotel where the relief workers were staying. Instead he was going to take her to his home. It was better that they didn't expose anyone else to possible infectious dysentery.

He'd sent Kariff out to warn the other farmers and plantation owners in that area who used that water source to avoid using water from the creek and he ensured the palace was made aware of the dire situation and that bottled, safe water would be provided to all who needed it.

He didn't say anything to Jeena as he drove back to Huban.

Thankfully he had also had a house that was not part of the palace. Maazin felt it was easier on his mother not to be under the same roof. So he'd chosen a colonial-built home just outside the city. He liked the privacy it afforded and what the two of them needed was privacy.

He was still in shock over the fact he had a son and he was going to find out who had kept this information from him and why. Maazin knew the mail and any correspondence to the royal family was monitored for their own safety, but he was so angry that someone could have done this.

His son.

His nine-year-old son. One that reminded him so much of his beloved brother Ali. Except the eyes. The eyes on that boy were his.

A son he didn't deserve.

Ali's family had been taken from him and it was a cruel twist of fate that he, the one responsible for Ali's death, had a son.

"Where are we going? I thought the hotel was near the hospital?" Jeena asked, her voice rising in panic.

"It is, but I don't think it's safe that we stay close to the field hospital for the next twenty-four hours, so I'm taking you back to my place."

Her eyes widened. "Oh, I don't think so! I'm not going to the palace. You need to stop this vehicle right now."

"What is wrong?"

"I'm not going to the palace."

"I never said we were." And he couldn't help but wonder why she was so worried about going to the palace.

"You said we were going to your home."

"I don't live in the palace."

She looked at him in disbelief. "Right."

"No, really I don't. I bought a colonial home just outside the city. It was the old British consulate. It's walled and gated, so pretty secure. My father thought maybe letting me have my own place would curb some of my less desirable behavior."

"Did it?" she asked.

"No, not right away…" It wasn't the house that had given him a taste of being a responsible adult, it was the unbearable heartbreak Jeena had caused him by leaving him without any explanation and Ali's death.

Maazin had blood on his hands as far as he was concerned. And since Ali had died, he'd been trying so hard to right all his wrongs.

He hadn't had a drop to drink for ten years, but right now he felt like getting drunk.

Jeena seemed to calm down again once he assured her that they weren't headed to the palace. He turned off the main promenade that led to the palace and headed down the road toward the beach.

His home had sustained a bit of damage, but Maazin had made sure everything had been made secure when he'd known that the cyclone would definitely hit. He'd moved out all his staff and this was the first time he'd been back after Blandine. He'd been so busy with helping his people that he hadn't even thought about his home.

He parked the Jeep and then hopped out.

"Where are you going?" Jeena asked.

"The power to the gate has been cut. All power is being diverted to essential services only. Luxury items like powered gates are not essential." He unlocked the gate and then pushed on it to open it.

Once it was open he climbed back into the Jeep and drove it inside, then parked and repeated the process to close the gates.

He was relieved to see that only a few boards had been taken off and just one of the shutters was broken.

There were some fallen trees, but the larger ones still stood and no branches or trees had fallen on his house.

Jeena climbed out of the vehicle and looked at his home. "It's nice. I like the cerulean blue. It reminds me of the ocean."

He nodded. Pleased that she liked it. "It's what I was going for. This place is peaceful and it's nice to come here and not be a prince."

"I'm sure it's so very taxing." She walked past him, her arms crossed as she looked all around his garden. He wasn't sure if she was commiserating with him or being sarcastic, but had a feeling it might be a mix of the two.

And he didn't care. He was going to make her a simple meal out of the supplies he had in the house and then he was going to find out more information about his son.

He climbed up the steps onto the covered deck and prised off the wooden boards and then unlocked the door.

"Right this way, Dr. Harrak."

Jeena followed him into the hallway and he flicked on the light, glad he'd had backup generators installed last year.

There was a bit of water pooling on the marble floor, but for the most part everything looked to be in the same place as before the cyclone had hit.

"Wow, so this was the British Consulate?"

"It was moved to downtown Huban, but this is where the British had a seat for many years. Colonialism at its finest. Why don't you make yourself comfortable in the sitting room and I'll see what I have to eat."

Jeena nodded and found her way to the front sitting room. It was a cool room that he liked to use in the heat of the summer as it got breezes from the ocean and didn't have the direct sun.

In the kitchen there were bananas, which had gone bad, on the counter, so he tossed them and cleaned up the marble counter top so as not to attract insects or vermin, and then he looked in the fridge, which was still running.

He had absolutely no idea what to make.

He might like his independence, but he had staff who cooked and cleaned for him. When he'd been in England for medical school, his father had made sure that he'd been well taken care of and had wanted for nothing.

Even when he'd been serving in Kalyana's military and continuing his medical training to be an army surgeon, he'd had servants.

He knew how to make a few things, but he really didn't want to make toast for Jeena.

"Is everything okay?" she asked, peeking into the kitchen.

"No. I… Fine," he said, throwing up his hands. "I'm a pampered, coddled prince and I don't know how to make you anything that might be slightly edible. I can make toast and a pot of tea. Would you like that?"

Jeena bit her bottom lip, trying not to smile.

He'd always found that endearing, but right now he was slightly annoyed.

"Let's see what you have." She padded over to the fridge. "You have enough to make a nice Greek salad. Tomatoes, feta and olives. Would you like that?"

"That sounds wonderful." Now he was smiling and couldn't help but chuckle. "Would you show me?"

"How to make a salad?"

He nodded. "Yes."

"Sure." She pulled tomatoes, cucumber, feta and olives from the fridge and then wandered over to the pantry and pulled out olive oil, vinegar and oregano. He hadn't realized that he'd had all these things.

"Don't you need lettuce?" he asked. "It is a salad."

"If you want a traditional Greek salad then you don't have lettuce. You wouldn't happen to have any lemons, would you?"

"Yes, here you go." He handed her a couple. "Can we add lettuce too?"

"Why?" she asked.

"I like it and I think it might go bad soon."

Jeena wrinkled her nose. "Okay, let's see what we can salvage of it, but you know now it's not a true Greek salad."

"I'm sure I'll survive," he teased, pulling out the head of lettuce.

Jeena got to work and was washing the salad ingredients with bottled water. "Perhaps you should boil some water. If you're under a boiled water advisory, it would be safe."

"I have a lot of bottled water. I'm prepared for emergency situations. They wouldn't let a prince living on his own be without the essentials."

"Oh, good." Jeena finished what she was doing and then pulled out a cutting board and knife. "Do you have a big bowl?"

"Probably," Maazin said lightly. He went hunting through the cupboards until he found a large bowl. "Will this do?"

Her eyes widened. "That's massive, I'm sure it'll do."

"Too big?" he asked, glancing at it.

"For the two of us, yes, unless you have someone else coming over?"

He noticed there was a hint of apprehension in her voice and he wanted to ask her what she was so afraid of. First she'd been afraid of going to the palace and now she was worried about who else could be coming.

Did she know about the arranged marriage?

Of course she does. Who in the world doesn't?

The only thing people didn't know about was how the engagement was off and he couldn't tell anyone yet. He'd promised his father that. The people had loved Lady Meleena, or at least the idea of a fairy-tale wedding, not knowing that she was a spoiled and self-centered woman. Her father was from the Kalyanese dynasty, but they no longer lived in Kalyana and had made their home in Dubai. The last time Maazin had seen Meelena had been over a year ago. She'd been fed up that he'd chosen duty over her. But he'd never fancied Meleena. They'd been first introduced at that same polo match where he'd met Jeena, but the moment he'd seen Jeena all other women had paled in comparison...

"*Your Highness,*" Meelena said.

She was very beautiful, but he could tell she was less than impressed to meet him. There was no spark or zest for life in her eyes and she seemed bored. Like every other debutante in his social circle.

Maazin bowed. "Excuse my dishabille."

She looked him up and down with no interest. "You're playing a match. I would expect nothing less."

Maazin tried to think of something else to say, but he couldn't. She turned and sipped her champagne and made it clear that she didn't really want anything to do with him.

Did his father really expect him to marry Meelena? She was not his choice and never would be.

His eyes then fell on a beautiful woman in the most stunning emerald dress and ridiculous heels on the polo field.

Meleena followed his gaze. "What a fool," she snorted derisively.

"Excuse me," Maazin said quickly, and strode across the pitch to help her.

"So making a salad is extremely complicated, Your Highness," she teased, interrupting his thoughts.

"Oh?" he asked, crossing his arms.

"Yes." She smiled brightly at him and any tension that was between the two of them melted away. It was so easy with Jeena.

Why did she have to leave?

"You chop the lettuce iike this."

He rolled his eyes and stifled a laugh. "Can I try?"

She handed him the knife and he cut the lettuce.

"You've done this before," she teased again.

"I'm not completely helpless," he said dryly.

"Just a moment ago you said the opposite, Your Highness."

"Call me Maazin."

A blush tinged her high cheeks. "I can't do that."

"Why?" he asked.

"It's not right. It's not proper."

"Well, we're alone."

"So?" she asked, nervously.

"You can call me Maazin. Please. I prefer it."

She glanced at him. "Fine, but only because we're alone."

He chuckled softly and finished chopping the lettuce and dumped it into the bowl. "Now what?"

"Let's chop the tomatoes." She handed him one.

He tried to chop it up correctly but ended up butchering it, spreading seeds and juice everywhere. Jeena chuckled and took the knife back.

"How about you go change and I'll finish here?"

Maazin nodded. "It's probably for the best."

As he left the kitchen there was a knock at his front door. Maazin cursed under his breath and went to answer the door.

"Yes?" he said, not thinking and opening the door. Thankfully it was just Joseph Malliot, his father's aide-de-camp, standing on the doorstep. He looked worried.

"I'm sorry for disturbing you, Your Highness. I went to the makeshift hospital and was told that you and another doctor had left."

"Yes, we were potentially exposed to dysentery. We have to be isolated for the next twenty-four hours, it's highly contagious."

Joseph worried his bottom lip and then stepped forward. "Your father got wind that it's a female physician staying with you and he's concerned about your upcoming marriage to Lady Meleena. Or rather…"

"That the doctor will find out and let it slip to the press that I'm no longer engaged to Lady Meleena."

Joseph nodded. "Yes, Your Highness."

"That's why he sent you to the camp?"

"Well, no. He wanted you back at the palace. Your mother is still a little concerned that you're working out there alone and without any kind of protection."

Maazin sighed. "I'm glad she's worried about my safety, but I can assure you that there is nothing untoward between myself and the other doctor. You can tell them I'm safe at my home and once I'm sure I'm not contagious then I will come and see them and assure them of these things myself."

Maazin shut the door on Joseph. He didn't meant to be rude, but he didn't want Joseph to get ill. His father would be lost without Joseph at his beck and call.

And if Joseph got sick because of him, it would just be one more thing his mother could blame him for.

"If it wasn't for your reckless ways then Farhan wouldn't have had to come back and step up as the next in line. I had been training Ali to be King since his birth. He was ready to be a great king. But because of your foolish ways he's dead."

Maazin swallowed the lump in his throat and his stomach twisted, he felt like he was going to be sick.

He was a failure.

He had killed his brother. The woman he loved had left and his son didn't even know he existed. It was too much to deal with and his eyes drifted to the locked bar, which he knew was stocked, but he turned his back on it. He wasn't going back down that path.

Not again.

CHAPTER FOUR

JEENA HAD FINISHED making the salad, but there was no sign of Maazin returning and she was worried. What if he'd passed out?

What if something had happened to him? She crept out of the kitchen and made her way into the hall.

The large colonial house was eerily quiet.

And then she heard faint grunts coming from the far side of the house. She found another hall off the dining room, past the library and into what looked like a home gym.

Maazin had stripped off the scrubs and was in shorts and sneakers. He wasn't wearing a shirt and Jeena was taken aback. She knew that he was in good shape, but she wasn't prepared to see him standing there and doing a deadlift. The sweat dripped down his back and all of his muscles bulged as he arched his back and lifted what looked like a lot of weight.

His eyes focused on her standing in the doorway in the mirror he was facing. He finished his lift and then dropped the weights with a large clang on the mat.

"Jeena?" he said, surprised to see her there.

"You didn't come back," she said. "I was worried that maybe you fainted or were in distress."

"No, sorry. I was just... I needed to blow off some steam." He grabbed a towel and wiped his face.

And she couldn't blame him for blowing off some steam. She could do with some of that. She hadn't even been in Kalyana twenty-four hours and already her world was being turned upside down.

"There's some salad in the kitchen for you. I'm hoping you have a room for me and maybe I could have a quick shower? I feel pretty gross after that flight from Canada to Dubai and then here, then having to deal with dysentery."

"Of course. I'll take you to the guest room and I'll make sure you have a change of clothes."

"You keep women's clothing around?" And then she realized that was a stupid thing to say. Everyone knew that he was engaged to Lady Meleena. It had been announced to the world. Why they still weren't married was a mystery. Three years was a long engagement.

How would you know?

The Crown Prince Ali's death and Maazin's military service probably had something to do with it. But whatever the reason, it should not concern her. She would do well to remember that. Maazin had chosen Lady Meleena over her. He hadn't loved her at all and had made his feelings pretty clear when he hadn't come for her or fight for their love, even though he'd known she'd been pregnant. She was probably the only one who'd been in love in the first place.

"No, I don't have women's clothing on hand, but I can lend you one of my kurtas while your clothes are washed."

"I would appreciate that. Thank you."

Maazin nodded and led the way out of his gym and back out into the main foyer and up the stairs. He led her to a room that was above the gym and opened the door.

"This is the guest room and there's a private bath. It's the nicest guest room as it's under a shade tree and faces the pool out back. Though, until we're cleared of any in-

fection, I wouldn't advise a dip in the pool.
In the closet you'll find some plain kurtas
that will fit you."

She nodded. "Thank you, Your Highness."

His expression softened. "Just Maazin.
Please."

And it was sincere and gentle.

She nodded. "Maazin. Thank you."

He nodded and then left the room, closing the door behind him. Jeena let out a sigh
of relief that she hadn't known she'd been
holding. She walked over to the window and
peered outside. The sun was beginning to
set, the brilliant orange-gold light reflecting
off the infinity pool that seemed to melt into
the cerulean-blue ocean horizon.

Jeena sighed again.

She pulled out her phone and saw that she
had an attachment of pictures. She opened
it, not caring about the roaming charges
at the moment, and smiled when she saw
pictures her father had taken of Syman's
hockey game.

Some were blurry, but there were a few
good ones.

And there was a sweet one of Syman and
her father after the game, enjoying a slice
of pizza. Then there was a picture of Syman

and her mother. Her mother was tucking Syman into bed and there was a caption that said they all missed her and loved her. Tears welled in her eyes.

She missed them too.

And she knew that her mother and father were very worried for her sake. Jeena couldn't help but wonder what would have become of her parents had they still been on the plantation. How would they have fared?

Would they have gotten sick like that boy and his father?

Would her mother have died from a farming accident?

Why was that family still getting their water from the creek?

Maybe it was good that her family gone to Canada. Canada had been good to them. Her father had learned how to farm in Alberta and had a small ranch of his own. Instead of vanilla, he'd built greenhouses and cultivated flowers.

Her mother would do flower arrangements and Jeena was a surgeon. Syman may not be able to experience the same childhood she'd had, but he still had so many opportunities.

And he was living on a farm, just a different one from the one she'd grown up on, and the best thing of all was that he was free to choose who he loved.

Who he married.

There was no protocol that decided his life for him.

Until now.

Jeena worried her bottom lip. Maazin knew about Syman and she couldn't help but wonder what he'd do with that information. There was no more denying it. Would Syman be harassed by the tabloids? He was illegitimate, but he was Maazin's son nonetheless.

Prince Ali hadn't produced any children with his late wife. Farhan didn't have any children, not yet anyway. Maazin had a son.

Syman was an heir, even if he had been born out of wedlock.

Yeah, but Maazin doesn't seem too interested in knowing about his son now, does he?

And Maazin was due to wed Lady Meleena. She had no doubt that Meleena would do her duty and produce a legitimate heir.

Until that time, though, Jeena was going to hold her breath and hope that Maazin didn't tell King Uttam about Syman's existence.

She couldn't lose Syman to Kalyana.

Jeena cursed under her breath.

She hoped that neither of them got sick, because she wanted to put as much distance between her and Maazin as possible, return to Canada and forget that she'd ever came back to the home that had turned its back on her.

Maazin paced and he was feeling a bit nervous, waiting for Jeena to come downstairs. He'd thought about this moment so many times. What he would say to her, but now that she was actually here, he didn't know what to say.

And they had a child together.

He felt deprived of that. It angered him.

Why did she hide it from me?

And he couldn't help but think it was because he was such a bad influence. He was the black sheep of the family. The rogue. The troublemaker.

Before Ali's death, he hadn't partied as hard as his family had always believed, he'd just wanted them to think that at the time so they wouldn't rely on him. So that he could be himself, so he could trick himself into believing that he was free.

He had, after all, been the third son at the time.

There hadn't been much expectation on him to settle down and produce an heir. And that had been fine by him. Then he'd met Jeena and had started to think about settling down. Until she'd left him, and he'd decided to actually live like everyone believed he'd lived. That's why Jeena had left him, so he'd indulged, just a hundred times worse than he should have.

Then Ali had died.

And Maazin had understood the errors of his ways, but it had obviously been too late. Ali was dead and he'd driven Jeena off, with their child.

He had to show her that he'd learned from his mistakes.

That he could be responsible, and maybe she would let him see the boy. To get to know him.

Do you really deserve that?

It was clear by Jeena's actions that she had no intention of returning to Kalyana permanently and Maazin had to help his country. They had to rebuild Kalyana and then break the news that he wasn't marrying Lady Meleena.

He turned around and saw that Jeena was standing uncertainly in the doorway, wearing one of his white linen kurtas. Her long dark hair was braided over her shoulder and he swore he had never seen a more beautiful sight.

Even though she'd broken his heart by leaving him all those years ago, he still thought she was the most breathtaking woman he'd ever seen.

The years hadn't changed that.

His heart may have hardened and he may have accepted his fate as a servant to Kalyana, but that didn't change the fact that he was still enraptured by her refined beauty. He was drawn to her spirit. She was a like a breath of fresh air. Still, after all this time.

"Won't you have a seat?" Maazin said, motioning toward one of the chintz couches was in the formal sitting room. The formal sitting room still had that old-world feel of the British colonies to it.

It wasn't furnished to his taste, but he only used this sitting room for visiting dignitaries. If he had his way, he would go with minimalistic.

Jeena took a wary step into the room. "This room doesn't seem to belong to you."

The corner of his mouth quirked up. She knew him so well. "You're right, but my father wanted me to leave it alone as it's part of our history. Winston Churchill came here when it was still the British Consulate. Would you like some tea?"

She nodded. "I would like that."

Maazin slipped out of the room and into the kitchen to grab the tray where he'd already prepared the tea, adding some sliced lemon. He brought it out to her.

"I'm impressed," she said as he set the tray on the table between the two over-stuffed chintz sofas that were across from each other.

"With what?" he asked, handing her a cup and saucer.

"You're not completely helpless in the kitchen. You know how to put together a formal tea service."

He chuckled. "Well, teatime is still a thing here in Kalyana. I know it's not something that's done in Canada."

"We have tea."

"Do you have teatime? As in a meal?"

"No. Well, my parents do. They did continue with some of their old customs." She took a careful sip of her tea. "This is good."

"I know." He leaned back. "Your parents live in Canada now too?"

A strange expression crossed her face. "They do."

"They had a prosperous plantation."

"I know, but now they own a prosperous set of greenhouses just outside Calgary." Her eyes went wide and he could tell that she was annoyed that she'd let it slip. Let her location slip. He was relieved. Canada was a big country. You could get lost in a country that big.

"That's in Alberta, isn't it?" he asked.

"Yes," she said carefully, and set down her teacup. "Why?"

"I always wondered where you had disappeared to." He wanted to add, "when you left me all those years ago," but couldn't quite bring out the words to say it.

"Well, now you know. Just outside Calgary, but just outside Calgary is a large area."

"But given the agricultural industry of the Canadian prairies and indeed Alberta itself, how many large greenhouse operations are there in that area and how many grow and sell tropical flowers? Which I also find interesting, because I wouldn't think there was a big market for tropical flowers in Alberta."

Her dark eyes narrowed and he could tell that he was treading on dangerous ground.

"Poinsettias are tropical and need heat, but are much loved at Christmas, which is bitterly cold in Alberta."

"It's impressive they found such a niche market, but that's not surprising given that they left their home country with basically nothing."

Her lips pursed. "What does it matter? People leave all the time."

"Your family left behind their prosperous vanilla plantation. I know they sold that plantation for peanuts. Way under value. They took a significant hit financially and I know that your father is a savvy businessman."

"So?"

"So? That I did not understand. I did not understand why he would sell for next to nothing a plantation that had been in his family for generations."

Jeena stood to her feet. "My father had to sell our beloved family home. There was no choice. I was pregnant by a prince who couldn't care less. What choice did I have?"

He was floored by her anger. He hadn't known she was pregnant, but she was acting like he had known. "What do you mean, I couldn't care less? I didn't even know!"

She crossed her arms. "Your fiancée is the one who helped my family leave. She said that you knew and she gave me a check to take care of my costs."

Maazin saw red. "Meleena knew?"

Tears filled Jeena's eyes and she worried her bottom lip, nodding. "She did."

"I wasn't engaged to Meleena then," he said, but he was angry.

He knew that Meleena was manipulative, but he hadn't known this. It made sense now why she'd supposedly found the letter that Jeena had left.

"I'm aware of that and I always wondered if she was trying to get me out of the way so she could have you. I guess she won."

"She didn't win," Maazin said, shaking her head.

"You're engaged to her."

"No. No, I'm not."

Jeena's eyes widened. "What do you mean?"

"She's ended it and my father has kept it secret. There are some things to work out, but Lady Meleena ended it and I was quite relieved."

Jeena sat down slowly, looking a little pale.

Frankly, he was feeling a bit ill. Meleena had manipulated them both.

Still, that didn't bring back Ali or his wife. They were gone and Maazin still blamed himself for it all.

"So you really didn't know?" she whispered.

"No. I didn't. If I'd have known…" He trailed off, because he didn't know what to say. What if he had known? He would have gone after her? Of course he would have. He wished he had, not only for Jeena's sake but also for Ali and Chandni. But even if he hadn't gone out to that party, and Ali and Chandni hadn't died, he knew that the future for him, Jeena and their unborn child would still have been fraught with uncertainty. Would his family have accepted her? Would she have wanted this life? Would he have wanted his son to have the same life he'd had?

He wasn't sure.

But none of it mattered anyway. Ali and Chandni were dead, and he had to live with the guilt. Jeena and Syman had built a life in Canada that did not include him. And he had to accept that too.

It was too much to process and he felt awful. He hung his head.

"I think I need to rest," Jeena said quietly, her voice breaking slightly as if she was grappling with the same amount of emotion he was. "It's been a lot today."

He nodded. "I know."

She got up and left.

He didn't follow.

Maazin tossed and turned all night. It was all he could do not to go and see Jeena. He wanted to make things right, but he wasn't sure that he knew how.

It was early morning when finally he gave up any pretense of trying to fall asleep and got up, showered and dressed. When he got downstairs he found Jeena waiting calmly in the hall. She was dressed as well, in her now clean clothes. Her hair was braided back and she looked like she was ready to flee.

Again.

"Jeena?" he asked in surprise. "What are you doing up so early?"

"I need to get back to work. My team has been working all night and I've been lounging about here."

"You were hardly lounging about on purpose. We had to wait to make sure that neither one of us was infected."

"And we're not. We would've had symptoms by now, so I need to go back to work. My phone is dead, though, my charger is in my gear back with my team and your phone line is dead so I couldn't call a taxi to come and take me back to the makeshift hospital."

"The phone lines on this side of Huban are still out of order, but you wouldn't have been able to order any cab to come here and take you to the southeast district. No cab driver is equipped to handle that road. Only medical personnel and the army have permission to even try to traverse the roads."

Jeena sighed in resignation. "Will you take me, then?"

She didn't seem to want to rely on him. Not that he could blame her, he'd been hardly reliable in the past, but that was the past. This was different.

The only thing that wasn't different was

that Ali was dead and he was responsible. That was his burden to bear.

The past is the past.

He nodded. "I'll drive you, of course."

"Thank you."

Maazin came down the rest of the stairs and grabbed his keys. He opened the door for Jeena while he finished locking up his home. He wasn't sure when he would get back here again and until the roads were open outside the city he wasn't sure when his small staff would make it back here.

They drove away from his home and back toward the southeastern district in near silence. He didn't know what to say. She'd had his child and he hadn't been there. He hadn't known about it.

Unless Syman isn't yours?

No. Syman was his. He knew that without a doubt.

It was one of the things he'd adored about Jeena when they'd first met. She had been so different from all the women in his social circle. She had been honest and good.

Or at least he'd thought she was until she'd left him.

One thing he did know, he had to get to the bottom of this. After he'd made sure that

Jeena got back to the makeshift hospital and was reunited with her team, he was going to head straight to the palace and demand some answers from his parents.

"Have you heard from…?" He trailed off because it was hard for him to even think about the fact that he had a son. A son he knew nothing about.

There was so much he wanted to know about him but, then, there was so much he was afraid to know, and then there was a part of him that felt that maybe it would be better that Syman didn't know him or anything about this life.

Syman was currently free and he envied the boy that. Still, he was Syman's father and he wanted to know him.

You don't deserve to know him. You cost Ali his life. You don't deserve to have a child.

And he had to keep reminding himself of that.

"Syman?" she asked.

"Yes."

"I haven't heard from him since my phone died and I'm sure he's worried that he hasn't heard from me. I know my parents will worry."

Maazin nodded. "Well, they'll certainly

be relieved when you tell them that you didn't contract dysentery."

She smiled. "Of course."

He hated that there was this awkwardness between the two of them, but he was the one to blame for that. He'd foolishly believed that she'd written that letter. It was clear now she hadn't. He hated that the both of them had been manipulated by Meleena.

At least Jeena hadn't destroyed anyone's life. She started a new life in Canada and prospered. He'd wallowed in self-pity and had caused his brother's death.

"So, why did you agree to marry Meleena?" she asked.

He almost lost control of the car. "What?"

"Maazin, clearly you loathe her or rather loathed her. Why did you agree to marry her?"

He sighed. "I didn't loathe her. I didn't particularly care for her but 'loathe' is a strong word."

She cocked her head to one side, studying him. "Fine. So why? Why get engaged to her and then let the engagement go on for so long?"

Because I couldn't get over you.

"It's my duty to marry and…" He had

been going to say "produce an heir," but in reality he'd already done that. Illegitimacy aside, Syman was his heir.

Jeena's cheeks flushed with crimson. "I get it. You need a legitimate heir and, believe me, that's not why I wanted you to know about Syman. I don't need anything from you, Maazin. I haven't needed you."

That cut him to the quick.

I haven't needed you.

And he deserved it. He truly did.

No one really needed him.

Only his patients, which was one thing he never took for granted. His patients needed him, his people needed him and he would keep that promise he'd made all those years ago when Jeena had left and Ali had died, his promise to dedicate his life to his work and making sure everyone in Kalyana was taken care of.

Properly.

"Well, it doesn't matter now. It's done. The past is in the past," he said quickly.

He was done talking about this.

There was no point to discussing it further. The truth was out and even though Meleena had ruined a life with his son, it had been his own actions that had killed his brother and sister-in-law. Jeena was right. She didn't need him in her life, and he truly deserved it.

That was karma for you.

CHAPTER FIVE

I wish I had never said that to him.

It had been a couple of days since Jeena had last seen Maazin and had said those hurtful words that she was now regretting, even if they had been the truth.

She hadn't needed him in Canada. There were times she thought she did but, no, she didn't really need him. She was raising Syman to be a capable man.

And she'd learned that from the moment she'd walked through the doors of that first hospital in her intern year. A single mother in a foreign country. She'd had to rely on herself. Jeena had learned to rely only on herself.

Still, it wasn't his fault. He didn't know she had been pregnant. They had both been manipulated, but he didn't say whether he would've come to her aid. He'd trailed off, which made her believe he didn't want the responsibility.

Or that he was afraid of it.

And they weren't married. A prince had to produce a legitimate heir.

Still, she shouldn't have said that to him and she was regretting her words. She'd forgotten herself. When she'd been studying to be a doctor there'd been so many times that she'd had to really fight for her education. To be heard. Especially because she was a woman and she was a woman of color and an immigrant to Canada to boot. She'd had to become tough and fight for what she wanted and sometimes she was more brusque than she needed to be.

And that had been one of those times.

Maazin hadn't said much to her. He'd dropped her off so she could get checked out by her team and rejoin them in their relief work and then disappeared.

She would catch glimpses of him, but he was busy doing his work and wouldn't even look in her direction. He was acting like she wasn't even there.

It's for the best and what you wanted. He knows about Syman. You've done your part.

Which was true. From the moment she'd

known she'd be returning to Kalyana, she'd been terrified about running into him again, but now that it hadn't been as bad as she'd thought it was going to be, she liked being around him.

She'd forgotten how charming he could be.

His charm is why you got into trouble in the first place.

And as she watched him across the hospital, checking on his people and being so tender and gentle with the sickest and poorest of the Kalyanese people, it warmed her heart. This was a different man from the playboy who'd swept her off her feet.

He seemed at ease and he was putting the poorest of the poor above himself.

He cared about something. He seemed passionate about something, instead of just coasting, like he had before.

Maybe he had changed?

How much could a member of the Kalyanese royal family change, though? They were bound by protocol and restrictions. They had everything, yet they weren't free. Maazin had told her that many times when they'd been together.

He was bound by duty and Jeena was

very aware of the security personnel that surrounded the hospital. She didn't want this kind of life for Syman.

"So, you're the other Canadian Kalyanese doctor I've been told about."

Jeena startled and turned to see the bright smile of a beautiful woman, one who she recognized from photographs that had been plastered everywhere when Crown Prince Farhan Aaloui had wed his Canadian bride, Dr. Sara Greer.

"Your Highness." Jeena gave a small curtsey in deference to Sara.

A blush stained Sara's cheeks. "You don't need to do that."

"I do. I may be Canadian now, but I am Kalyanese and you are the Crown Princess. You will be my Queen one day."

"I'm really not used to all this bowing and scraping," Sara admitted. "I would like it if you just called me Sara."

Jeena nodded and smiled. "I would like that."

"Good," Sara said, relieved. "I was hoping that I was going to have a chance to run into you."

"Oh?" Jeena asked.

Sara motioned for them to head over to

a quiet area, out of earshot of any patients, and now Jeena wondered if she knew about Syman too.

"I was wondering how long your team was planning on staying here? I asked, but couldn't get any definitive answers from anyone."

Jeena relaxed. "Oh, well…our work visas have been cleared for us to remain for at least two weeks minimum, but given the state that Kalyana is in after this cyclone it could be longer."

"That's what I was hoping for."

Jeena raised an eyebrow. "You were hoping we'd stay longer?"

"Well, not for that reason. I have been speaking to Farhan about the need to promote women in STEM programs and encouraging Kalyanese women to pursue STEM as a career. Especially in medicine, but there's no university here so young people have to study abroad, and a lot of families can't afford to send their children off-island for education."

Sara was right. Jeena had always had an interest in science and medicine, but her parents hadn't been able to afford to send her to a school to study abroad, which had been the only option.

Even though they hadn't wanted to go to Canada at first, it had worked out and Jeena had got her education.

"How do I fit in?" Jeena asked.

"I thought we could get together and work on a proposal to support young women in studying medicine abroad and returning to practice here. I'd also like to explore the possibility of Kalyana having its own university. As someone who grew up here, I would love to pick your brains. And maybe then we could speak to young women and inspire them. Let them know there are options for them. Both of us are successful Kalyanese doctors." Sara smiled brightly. "It's all just a bunch of jumbled hazy thoughts in my head, but I would love your input."

Jeena smiled. "I think that's a great idea."

"Right?" Sara crossed her arms. "I knew that I would like you. You think like me."

"I appreciate that. I don't find many people who think like me. Of course, living in Alberta I was the only one from Kalyana."

"I understand that. Where I grew up in London, Ontario I didn't really run into people from our country either. Of course, I was adopted and for a long time didn't even know that I was Kalyanese."

"That's a shame," Jeena said, and then quickly corrected herself. "Not because you were adopted, but that you didn't know anything about Kalyana. It really is a wonderful country and I've missed it."

"Can I ask something else?"

Jeena knew what was coming and she wanted to say no, but she couldn't. "You want to know why I left?"

"Yeah, it's obvious you love it here so much."

"I do. I love my parents more and my father had an opportunity to make his dreams of becoming a tropical flower farmer a reality. There wasn't enough land to fulfill his needs in Kalyana, so he moved to Canada when the opportunity came. I'm their only child and I wanted to become a doctor. As you say, there isn't really opportunity here in Kalyana for young women to do that, so I went with them. I haven't regretted it and I'm glad to be back here and helping the country of my birth."

It was all a lie, but Sara didn't need to know the sordid details.

Sara smiled. "That's lovely."

"Your Highness?"

Sara spun around to see a security guard waiting. She bit her lip and then turned back to Jeena. "I have to go. It was wonderful to meet you, Dr. Harrak."

Jeena bowed her head. "The pleasure is all mine, Your Highness."

Sara left with the security guard and Jeena let out of a sigh of relief that she hadn't even known she was holding. She was so worried that Sara had been told about her past, that Sara knew about Syman that...well, she didn't know what.

She was just so worried that others would find out about her and Syman. No one needed to know that Maazin was Syman's father.

Jeena had the feeling that someone was staring at her and she glanced over to see that Maazin was looking at her with curiosity.

Don't think about him.

She turned back to her work. He had made it clear that he was mad at her and she'd said something she completely regretted, but maybe this was for the best.

He leaned over, his breath on her neck

making a tingle run down her spine. "I see that you've met Sara."

"I thought you weren't talking to me, Your Highness?" she replied.

"Yes, well I was curious when I saw Sara come in and introduce herself."

Jeena sighed. "Look, about what I said…"

He held up his hand. "I don't want to talk about that. What did Sara want?"

"She wanted me to help with her initiative to promote the STEM programs to young women in Kalyana. I told her that I would back her on that. Help her with her ideas for her proposal. Talk to other young women interested in the sciences."

"You're not here for long, how can you?" he asked, crossing his arms. "For that matter, why did she ask you to participate in this?"

"She asked me because I am Kalyanese and even though her heritage is Kalyanese, she was born in Canada and feels that I would have a better perspective of the needs here, as I grew up here."

Maazin cocked an eyebrow. "I can see that."

"I'm glad," she replied saucily. "Was that all you wanted to discuss?"

"Actually, there's a medical emergency on a small island north of Agung and I could use your help. We can take the royal yacht, which is loaded with supplies, and go and treat the village that has been cut off since Blandine hit."

Even though she knew it wasn't a good idea to be alone with Maazin and on his yacht, no less, she couldn't turn her back on patients who needed her.

"Okay." She nodded and set down the chart she was working on. "When do you want to leave?"

"Within the hour. Gather what gear you need, in case we have to stay overnight. I'll make the other arrangements and have a car come and get you to bring you down to the harbor." He turned and left before she had a chance to protest, before she had a chance to change her mind.

This is not a smart idea.

But, really, this was part of her mission to Kalyana.

She really didn't have a choice. This was what she was here for.

Maazin did the final checks on the yacht. Soon Jeena would arrive and he would set out on the hour-long sail to the island north of Agung. He would rather take the helicopter, but there was nowhere to land safely on the small island of Petrie because Blandine had damaged it so badly.

"Sara mentioned that you were getting your yacht ready to head out to Petrie."

Maazin glanced down onto the dock and saw that Farhan was standing there. Off in the distance were the security guards, ever-present when the Crown Prince was around.

"I am." Maazin walked onto the dock. "Is there an issue with that?"

Farhan shrugged. "Mother isn't happy about it. She thinks that you should send one of our doctors who is not royal blood, or the relief workers. You know Mother and how she worries."

Do I?

It didn't seem to him his mother cared much for him. Not since Ali had died. He knew his mother blamed him. She barely acknowledged him. It cut him to the quick. He'd managed to make his peace with his father. If only he could make things right with his mother, but he doubted that would ever happen. She was too hurt, too distant, and he felt responsible.

Actually, he was responsible.

He was certain she viewed him as a disappointment.

"You quite all right?" Farhan asked, cocking his head to one side. "You look out of sorts."

"I'm fine. A bit tired. I'm sure you heard about my little exposure to dysentery the other day."

"Yes. I did and don't worry, all that is being taken care of. The farmers in that area have been supplied with clean water and proper sanitation is in place."

"I'm glad to hear that."

"I know it's been a bit of an effort and difficult, but with the help of our allies we're getting the help that we need."

Farhan was ever the diplomat and Maazin had no doubt that he would be a great king one day. Even though it was Maazin's fault that Farhan had been put in that position in the first place.

"Did you want something else?" Maazin asked. "The other doctor will be here soon and we'll need to get going if we're to make Petrie Island before nightfall."

Maazin didn't mean to be so curt with Farhan, but he didn't want his brother around when Jeena arrived. Not that Farhan even knew who Jeena was. He hadn't told anyone about Jeena. The only ones who knew about her and the history he had with her were his mother and Lady Meleena apparently. No one else knew.

And no one needed to know about it.

Still, he didn't want Farhan meeting her and saying something to their father. And given the nature and turmoil that Kalyana was currently in, he wasn't sure how he was going to start that conversation.

"What, who, me?" Farhan asked.

"You didn't come here to see me off," Maazin said plainly.

"Fine. Mother wants you to return to the palace and Father is giving in to her." Farhan rubbed the back of his neck. "He says you don't need to be here."

Maazin could tell that Farhan felt uncomfortable telling him this.

Maybe go with Farhan and appease your mother?

Only he didn't want to. He'd promised to take Jeena to Petrie Island and this was part of his duty to his people. There were Kalyanese on Petrie Island who had lost everything and were in dire need. They needed him.

And that trumped his need to please his father.

"I can't," Maazin said quickly. "I promised those displaced people that I would take help and I will be there. Do you not think that's the right thing to do?"

Farhan sighed and nodded, rolling his shoulders. "I do."

"Thank you."

"Well, at least I tried, but..." Farhan trailed off and looked uncomfortable. "When you return I strongly urge you to return to the palace. Father is not well at the moment and it would be good if you returned. He's been asking you to come back to the palace since Blandine hit and you've been avoiding him. You need to go and see him."

"I know." Maazin knew that his father was feeling poorly. With his condition and the cyclone devastating Kalyana, it hadn't been good for their father, but he had a hard time being around his family. It was better to keep them at a distance.

It was easier that way.

"Good luck on your trip. If you need anything, please call and I will send for assistance."

Maazin shook his brother's hand. "Thank you."

Farhan turned and walked over to the

dark SUV with tinted windows and Kalyana flags. A security guard held open the door for Farhan as he slipped into the back.

Maazin waved as the SUV drove away from the harbor.

Maazin knew there was security watching him, and he knew there would be an attaché of security following the yacht to Petrie, but Maazin didn't need as much of a detail as the Crown Prince did.

Of course, Ali had had just as much security and that hadn't helped him.

"You shouldn't have gone to that party. What were you thinking?" Ali lambasted him, yelling above the rain that was pouring down and the constant swish of the wiper blades. *"You left your security team behind. Do you know how foolish that was?"*

"So?" Maazin asked, but he could barely keep his head up. He didn't care much about anything. Jeena was gone and his pain wouldn't end.

"Don't be so hard on him, Ali," Chandni whispered gently. *"His heart is broken."*

"It doesn't matter. He's a prince. He should behave better."

Maazin snorted. *"I'm third in line to the*

throne and, unlike you, Ali, I can do whatever I want."

"Or whoever," Ali snapped back. "Honestly, Maazin, when will you grow up?"

Maazin was going to answer, but before he could there was a large bang and the world turned upside down and went black...

"Hey, you okay?"

Maazin jumped and realized that Jeena was standing beside him. He hadn't even seen her arrive. She carried a duffel bag and his security team was unloading medical supplies, as well as food and water from the back of the van that had replaced Farhan's SUV.

"Fine." Maazin scrubbed a hand over his face. "I'm okay. Sorry, I just zoned out."

"If you're sure…"

"I'm fine." Maazin turned away from her. "We'd better get loaded up and get on our way to Petrie before it gets too late."

He just had to put it all behind him.

He had to put the memory of Ali behind him, just like he had to put the memory of Jeena and how broken he'd been when she'd left behind him as well.

It was all in the past and, wish it as he

might, he couldn't go back and change anything.

The past was the past and his future was tied to serving his country and that was it. Maybe, just maybe then he could forgive himself for the damage he'd done.

Maybe.

CHAPTER SIX

THE WATER MADE Jeena a little nervous, but she felt safer being on Maazin's yacht and today was a beautiful, perfect day to be on the water.

Jeena raised her head to the sky and drank in the warmth of the late afternoon sun. Back in Calgary it was a bitter minus forty degrees Celsius and nothing like the beautiful eighty-degree weather that was here.

Just another thing she'd missed about Kalyana. She'd missed the warmth and sunshine. She was not a fan of winter or darkness. The only thing she liked about winter and darkness was the northern lights. That was something she was not sure she'd ever get tired of seeing.

She gazed out over the waters of the Indian Ocean, where all the islands that made up Kalyana lay. Beyond Kalyana lay the continent of Africa, Madagascar and then there was India, Yemen, Oman and the Maldives.

She'd forgotten what it was like to take a boat out to one of the far-flung islands of Kalyana. Looking east, she could make out the pearl-pink crescent of Patang Island.

On Patang Island had been the first time she had been with Maazin. She'd given her heart and soul to him that night, with no thought to the future and what it might hold for them.

Her cheeks heated as she thought of that night.

They had been on this yacht then too.

Their first time had been on the island, but then he'd carried her back to the yacht and made love to her again in his cabin. His arms around her, his hands in her hair and his mouth on hers. She'd been completely lost.

He'd been the only one to ever make her feel that way.

She'd been a fool.

And she had been such a fool to fall for a prince. What had she been thinking? She'd been so naive. So innocent. Well, she'd learned the hard way about trusting her heart to someone. The only one she could depend on was herself.

Jeena snuck a peak at Maazin at the helm, his white linen shirt billowing, his eyes focused on the horizon, and her pulse began to beat just a bit faster.

Damn him.

She hated that he still had an effect on her. Try as she might, she was still pulled toward him like a moth to a flame and she knew, just knew that if she allowed herself to get sucked in, she would get burned again.

This time she wouldn't let her heart lead her to disaster. When her work here was done she'd just leave and head back to Canada. There would be no struggle for her family. She wouldn't be as afraid. There was a life waiting for her in Canada. A damn good one.

Syman was her world and she was going to make sure that he was protected. She didn't want him sucked into this kind of life.

But Syman needs to know his father.

And it was that little voice she couldn't quell. Maazin deserved to know Syman and Syman deserved to know his father. She was just still afraid that Maazin would take Syman from her as Syman had royal blood.

It's what her parents feared. She couldn't lose Syman, but she couldn't deny a father and son.

Maazin looked at her. "You seem lost in thought."

"Not really lost in thought." It was a lie. She didn't want to tell him what she was really feeling. "Just enjoying the warmth and the sun."

"It's not really that warm."

"For me it is. It's bitterly cold in Canada. I'd forgotten how hot and wonderful the weather is here when the dark of winter hits."

"Dark of winter?" Maazin asked, raising an eyebrow. "Surely it's not that bad."

"Yes. It's that bad." Jeena pulled out her phone and scrolled through the photos to find the picture she'd taken when her father had had the laneway to the greenhouse plowed out a month ago during a bad blast of snow.

"Look at this." She got up and walked over to him, holding up her phone to show him the picture. He looked at it, raising his eyebrows.

"Wow," he said. "That's a lot of snow."

"Right. It gets so cold and dark." She exited the photo app. "There was so much snow and Syman was so mad that hockey had to be canceled for the night."

She closed her eyes and groaned inwardly. She hadn't meant to mention Syman again, but then again Maazin hadn't really asked much about him either.

"You've mentioned that he likes hockey," Maazin said. "Does he like other sports?"

"Baseball in the summer. Soccer as well."

"Football, you mean," Maazin said with a smile.

"Yes, I suppose European football is known as soccer there. He doesn't play American football. Though he is a fan of the Saskatchewan Roughriders, which is CFL over NFL."

"What's the difference?" Maazin asked. "Or is there one?"

"Oh, there's a difference, and people get really tetchy about it if you don't know."

He smiled, his eyes twinkling. "Do you know the difference?"

"Of course."

He cocked an eyebrow. "Well?"

"Well, what?"

"What's the difference?"

"Does it matter?" she asked.

"Yes." He smiled at her, a lazy half-smile. "Why?"

"Because," he teased. "You don't really know."

She chuckled. "Fine. I don't really know."

"So there's no difference, then?"

"Not really. I think it has something to do with field size. CFL is a bigger field size than NFL."

"Is there no cricket or polo in Canada?"

Jeena shrugged slightly. "They aren't really big in Canada."

"That's a shame. Perhaps…" He pursed his lips, as if he was going to offer to teach Syman cricket, but then thought better about it. It made her feel sad on one hand, but relieved as well. If he didn't want to be part of Syman's life or if he wasn't going to be around, she didn't want Syman to get hurt.

If he wanted out then he needed to say something.

She wasn't going to let Maazin hurt their son like he'd hurt her all those years ago.

Still, there was a part of her that wanted him to ask and know their son.

"You can ask me anything about him, you know. Anything you want," she said gently.

"I appreciate that."

She wanted to tell him that what she'd said the other day about not needing him didn't mean that she didn't want him to care about Syman. She just didn't want him to feel obligated to care for them, when he couldn't.

There was an almost palpable tension and she hated that it was so awkward around him. She remembered a time when it had been so easy between them. When they would talk for hours, laugh and make love.

Heat bloomed in her cheeks and she wandered to the starboard side of the ship to look out over the water. She leaned on the railing and sighed, trying not to think about the past, but everywhere she looked there it was. The past, calling to her.

Like a siren calling a doomed sailor to his death.

"You seem lost in thought again," Maazin said gently.

"Just…memories." She looked back at him. His expression was soft and he smiled at her, sending a thrill through her.

"I know. I was thinking the same thing. We took many a ride on this yacht."

"You liked the sea," she said.

"Don't you?" he asked.

"Yes… No. Water does frighten me. It's beautiful, but it's slightly terrifying."

"Then why did you come on yacht trips with me?" he asked.

"You liked it and I wanted to be with you."

He smiled gently at her, those gray-green eyes twinkling at her. "I thought you liked it and I wanted to please you."

"So you don't like it, then?"

"Yes and no. I like my yacht, but it wasn't because I liked cruising around on my own. I liked the privacy that it offered. Out here I can just be me. I'm not a prince. I'm no one."

She nodded. "I can understand that."

"I haven't asked much about Syman yet. I'm sorry. I'm processing it, but I want to know. I truly do."

"Look, I know I dropped this bombshell on you, but you had the right to know. I thought you did know."

"I understand. We were fooled."

She could hear the frustration in his voice.

"I am sorry."

"It's not your fault. And if I see her again…well, let's hope I don't."

"It's in the past," Jeena offered. Although she wouldn't mind taking a swift shot at Meleena.

"I am curious about one thing, though," Maazin said.

"What's that?" she asked.

"Why didn't you go to the press?" Maazin asked. "If you felt I hurt you, betrayed you, why didn't you tell the world what a vile, vicious man I was?"

"I'd never have done that. We were starting a new life away from Kalyana and didn't want to draw attention to ourselves. And I didn't want my child dragged into all of this. I didn't want him photographed or have the media follow us. There was so much going on when he was born. Your older brother Ali and his wife had died and—"

"I'm aware," Maazin said quickly, and a strange expression passed over his face. She had obviously touched a sore spot about Ali and she wondered what had happened. All she knew was that he and his wife had died in a car crash.

That was all anyone had ever been told.

"I'm sorry for your loss. I know how close you were to Ali."

Maazin nodded, but he wouldn't looked at her and she knew that whatever conversation they were having was over.

"For what it's worth, I'm not the kind

of person who would ever go to the press, Maazin. I would never hurt you like that."

He nodded, but didn't look at her. "Thank you."

She sat back down and focused on the ocean. Off in the distance she could see dark clouds rolling in. It was fitting for how she felt. For how Maazin obviously felt, given the tension between them.

Or at least it felt fitting.

For the rest of the trip to Petrie Island the atmosphere was tense. Jeena didn't say anything and neither did Maazin. The dark clouds were still in the distance, but Jeena had a real sense of foreboding as she watched them.

Even Maazin seemed on edge about it. As they approached the island Jeena gasped in shock. She remembered coming to Petrie Island with her grandfather a lot. He would sell vanilla on the island every Sunday and often take her.

The little island just north of the larger Agung was always bustling on a Sunday when the market came in.

There were other smaller islands all around the main island of Kalyana and all these small communities would come together and congregate on Petrie. They would share stories and sell their wares.

She remembered a weaver living on the island who would weave beautiful saris the color of the sea shot with gold. Her mother had one still.

But as they got closer to the island and Jeena could see the devastation, her heart sank. Houses had been toppled, trees uprooted and the small harbor that housed the islands' boats had been destroyed. Boats were capsized or washed ashore and irreparably damaged.

It was like a war zone.

It was awful.

Maazin pursed his lips and frowned. "It's worse than I thought."

"No one from Kalyana has been out this way since Blandine?" Jeena asked in shock.

"No. We've been unable to get here. There were so many wounded and sick on the main islands. Then those in further outlying areas were coming to the main island to seek help. No one from Petrie came, but now I understand why, they were unable to."

Maazin docked his yacht at the main pier, where police officers and first responders who lived on the island were waiting for his arrival.

Jeena's stomach twisted in a knot as she watched Maazin greet the men and women who were waiting for him. There was a lot of deference and saluting, but Maazin was quick to shut that all down.

"I've brought medical supplies," he told the man who Jeena assumed was the chief of police. "And a surgeon. This is Dr. Harrak."

Jeena climbed down onto the dock and shook everyone's hands.

"Jeena, this the chief of police on Petrie. His name is Mustafa. Mustafa, this is Dr. Jeena Harrak. She is Kalyanese, but is from Canada."

"We're so glad you've come, Your Highness," Mustafa said. "We have so many wounded. Our first aid and first responder teams have done what they can, but we have some who require surgical intervention."

"I'm here to help. Have all your buildings been damaged by the cyclone?" Jeena asked Mustafa.

"Not all. Those closest to the water have been. The city hall is standing as it was made from cement and cinderblock. We have moved all the wounded and sick there.

It's sheltered and has a generator." Mustafa looked exhausted. "We have an elderly gentleman who was brought to us last night by his daughter. He lived on one of the smaller islands. He was a weaver and one of our medics said he suspects that the man has appendicitis."

Jeena bit her lip. "That's not good."

"No, he's very ill. The medics have set him up with an IV antibiotic drip, but if it's appendicitis he really needs to get off island and have surgery."

"There might not be time to get him off island," Maazin stated.

"You're right. We'll have to check him." Jeena frowned. "I could perform an emergency surgery if I had to."

"Can you?" Mustafa asked, surprised.

"Of course. It's what I'm trained for," Jeena replied. "You said the man was a weaver?"

Mustafa nodded. "Yes, and a tailor, the only one in Petrie. He's been selling his fabrics, saris, kurtas and lenghas here for over twenty years. He's very talented."

Jeena smiled. "Yes. My mother has one of his saris. She cherishes it."

Mustafa grinned. "Harrak is your sur-name?"

"Yes."

"Is your grandfather Rami Harrak?" Mus-tafa asked.

"Yes, that was my grandfather. My father took over his plantation, until…" She trailed off, trying not to think about the night she and her family had left their home. "My par-ents live in Canada now."

"Good for them," Mustafa said, and Jeena was thankful he didn't ask any further ques-tions. "I'll take you to my truck and get you over to the courthouse. My other officers will make sure all your gear and supplies get there too."

Jeena nodded and then glanced at Maazin, who was staring at her with an unreadable expression on his face. She looked away quickly.

She didn't want to share that pain with him.

One for which she had blamed him for so long when it hadn't been his fault.

The drive to the courthouse that had been converted into a makeshift hospital didn't take too long. There wasn't much flooding and any rubble from the houses near the coast of the island had been cleared away. As had the trees. There were tents and a sort of makeshift shanty village the closer they got to the center of the town where the market was.

"Thankfully our water supply wasn't disrupted as it comes from a natural spring and because of our generator we're also able to have our desalinator up and running," Mustafa mentioned offhandedly as he drove through the streets.

"I'm glad. There was a small outbreak of dysentery on the main island that we were able to control," Maazin said. "I'm glad there is nothing like that here."

Jeena was glad too. Something like dysentery or another infectious disease would wreak havoc on the close-knit community of Petrie Island.

It didn't take long for them to get to the courthouse.

"We're here and I'll take you right to our most urgent patient, Mr. Patel." Mustafa parked and Jeena grabbed her duffel bag, which carried an emergency surgery kit. Something she always carried with her when she was going off into disaster zones.

Maazin followed Mustafa and Jeena followed them.

The medics had done a great job setting up the makeshift medical center. Jeena was impressed, but right now she wanted to take a look at Mr. Patel.

"He's in here. Our paramedic is with him."

"Thank you, Mustafa," Maazin said.

"Your Highness." Mustafa bowed.

Maazin held open the door for Jeena and she walked into the room. She could tell the man was very ill.

"Your Highness," the paramedic said with a curtsey.

"Please, it's okay. Can you tell us about Mr. Patel?" Maazin asked.

The paramedic nodded. "Mr. Patel was brought in early this morning. His daughter said he was complaining of lower right quadrant abdominal pain. Upon palpation we noticed he was guarding and his temperature was one hundred and two. He has been unable to pass a bowel movement and his blood test came back with a high count of white blood cells."

"So he's fighting an infection," Jeena said. She walked over to the bed and examined the patient. Mr Patel was just as she remembered him, slightly older, but he still looked the same.

"Yes," the paramedic said. "With antibiotics we've managed to bring his temperature down a bit, but it's rising again."

"Without an ultrasound it's pretty hard to tell if it's definitely appendicitis," Jeena said. "But from the description, it's not dysentery."

"There's no blood or mucus," the paramedic said. "It was our worry too, but Mr. Patel's daughter said he's been drinking bottled water. He's not a stranger to cyclones and storms."

"You've done an excellent job here," Jeena remarked, and she continued her examination. "You wouldn't happen to have certification in anesthesia, would you?"

The paramedic's eyes widened. "No."

"I do," Maazin said.

"That's good, but I do need someone to assist me."

"I can help with that. I'm training to be a surgical nurse," the paramedic said. "It's just been hard to get to a school, it's so costly..."

Jeena understood that only too well. There was no medical school in Kalyana and going abroad was very expensive, which was why her dream of becoming a surgeon hadn't been realized until she'd been banished and had moved to Canada.

"What's your name?" Jeena asked gently.

"Ayesha."

"Well, Ayesha, if you think you have a good handling of surgical instruments I would gladly have you assist me while Prince Maazin does the anesthesia."

"Thank you, Dr. Harrak."

"Please go prep a sterile room so that we can operate on Mr. Patel immediately."

"Of course." Ayesha left the room and Jeena went straight to her duffel bag to pull out her surgical kit.

"Are you sure this is wise?" Maazin asked, and she could hear the concern in his voice.

"If we don't do it, he won't survive the trip back to the main island. We have to."

"But with a paramedic assisting you?"

"She was smart enough to set up the IV and take his blood. You heard her, she wants to be an operating room nurse, a scrub nurse, but there's no little or no support available for her. This is what Sara was talking to me about so earnestly."

"I agree more could be done," Maazin said. "But this is a man's life."

"Exactly. I can do this, you'll be in the room and Ayesha is more than capable of assisting me."

Maazin looked uncertain. "What choice do we have? You're right. Very well, I'll be there and we can do this."

Jeena touched his arm. "Yes, we can do this."

Mr. Patel started to rouse and looked a bit surprised. "Your Highness?"

Maazin smiled at the man. "Mr. Patel, we're here to help you."

"Help me?" the patient asked, confused.

"You have appendicitis and Dr. Harrak from Canada and myself are going to take care of you."

Mr. Patel nodded and looked over at her. He smiled at her. "I recognize you."

Jeena smiled down at him. "I would say so. I saw you every weekend when I was a child."

"You are not Canadian," Mr. Patel said.

"I am now, but I'm back home to work and to help."

Mr. Patel closed his eyes. "Good. Good."

Jeena checked his pulse rate, which was

racing. "We need to get him into surgery now."

If they didn't, Mr. Patel was going to get peritonitis and die.

Maazin thought that Jeena was foolish thinking about operating on Mr. Patel in a makeshift hospital on the small island of Petrie with a paramedic as her assistant and without ultrasound assistance or other specialized equipment to do the surgery.

Ayesha had done a great job in prepping a small, well-lit room. Jeena's instinct was right and Mr. Patel's appendix was on the verge of rupturing, which would have meant a bad case of peritonitis, and as he was over seventy, his chances for survival in a disaster situation like this would not have been good without surgery.

Maazin felt bad for wanting to wait to transport him to Huban. He wouldn't have made that journey.

Now, here they were in a small courtroom and they were saving a man's life. Not only that, Jeena was inspiring a young Kalyanese paramedic who had aspirations of doing so much more. Jeena was wonderful. There was no other word to describe it.

He couldn't help but smile from behind his surgical mask as he watched her.

She was so strong and she didn't even know it.

Or she hadn't known it when they'd been together. She had changed. She was fierce and it made him want her all the more.

You can't have her.

And that thought replayed over and over in his mind as he watched Jeena work and explain things to Ayesha as they removed the enflamed appendix and cleaned out the infection from Mr. Patel's abdomen.

He was also jealous of Jeena.

She had more hands-on practical knowledge than he did. Maazin had training and he'd done work in the field, but rarely. His father ruled Maazin's schedule and there wasn't much time to really practice medicine or teach it. He may have been a military surgeon, but he didn't get to practice as much as he'd like to. As much as she obviously did.

He'd moved away from medicine into politics and diplomacy, something Maazin hated more than anything.

If he'd not been born into the royal family, if he'd had the same freedom as Jeena, then she would've never left Kalyana. They would be together, married, and Syman would know who he was.

A lump formed in his throat as he thought about Syman. A boy who loved sport as much as he did. Not that he knew anything about ice hockey, but he could learn.

That's if Jeena would let him get to know Syman. He was so afraid Jeena wouldn't let him. She'd offered to talk about him, but he didn't quite believe she was actually going to tell him about Syman. She was determined to protect their son, and he understood why.

Maazin lived his life in the spotlight as a member of the royal family. Nothing of his was private. His whole life was on display.

Even if he did meet his son, he wouldn't want to burden him with this life. This horrible public life that he couldn't escape. That he was bound to forever, not only by birth but by his mistakes, which had made him second in line to throne until Farhan had an heir.

Still, he was a father. There was duty there. He'd never thought of having children, but now he had one he had to do the right thing by him.

He had to prove to Jeena that he could.

Do you deserve a second chance?

No. He didn't and that thought sobered him up.

"Now let's close up," Jeena remarked.

"This is an amazing opportunity, Dr. Harrak. Thank you," Ayesha said.

"You're very welcome and thank you for assisting me."

"Yes. Thank you, Ayesha," Maazin said, finally finding his voice.

"Thank you, Your Highness," Ayesha said nervously.

They finished closing up Mr. Patel and Ayesha promised to monitor him post-op so that Jeena and Maazin could go out and assess the rest of the Petrie Island villagers who had been hurt during the cyclone.

Jeena washed up and disposed of the scrubs and then placed the instruments in a biohazard container that was filled with antiseptic.

"That's a handy kit you had," Maazin commented as he cleaned up.

"This isn't my first time heading to a disaster area. Of course, this is my first one out of Canada."

"What have you dealt with in Canada?" Maazin asked.

"Mostly things like accidents or avalanches in the mountains. Sometimes a hiker falls down a cliff and you have to attend out in the field."

"Avalanches?" Maazin asked in amazement.

"Or mudslides. I know Kalyana has had its fair share of those." She shuddered then and shook her head as if shaking away a bad memory.

"Why are you shuddering?"

She sighed. "When I was a child, I was almost swept out to sea by a flash flood during a particularly bad rainstorm. It terrified me, but I've overcome that fear. Still, every once in a while when I think about it, the terror comes right back."

So that's why she isn't fond of water.

"I'm sure," Maazin said quietly. He knew exactly what she was talking about. There were times when that accident came back to mind, flooding back, and it sent him into a tailspin. He hated the helpless feeling that came with it.

He hated being reminded of that horrible night and its aftermath. How his parents had everything hushed up. People had been paid off and no one knew Maazin had been drunk and fighting with Ali as Ali had been driving during a rainstorm.

No one knew Maazin was the reason Ali was dead.

He was the shame of his family.

"You okay?" she asked.

"I'm fine. And I will help."

"I assumed you would," Jeena teased. "You are a doctor too, Your Highness."

"I don't have as much practice in the field as you."

"Aren't you an army surgeon?" she asked.

He nodded. "Yes, but royal duties outweighed a lot of my opportunity for really getting out there and saving lives. Though I lend a hand when I can, still it would be nice to have the freedom that you have. I would like to learn more."

"That's too bad."

"What is?" he asked.

"That you're so trapped by that royal title."

"It is. I much prefer my medical work and working with people to protocol and diplomacy."

She nodded. "Still, with your power you could advocate for change. I admire that power you have to make a real difference."

"I can do that. Yes. And I plan to."

"You do?" she asked.

He smiled at her. "I mean, with Sara's initiative to promote STEM sciences and medical sciences, in particular to women, and to bring a university to Huban. Kalyana needs this. I think you should help her and I will too."

Jeena smiled brightly, her lovely dark eyes twinkling with that sparkle he hadn't seen in so long. "You will?"

"It's clear that something needs to be done. You did a wonderful job with Ayesha and you saved Mr. Patel's life."

"Thank you."

"Now, let's go and help some others."

"Good idea." Jeena grabbed her medical kit and they left the small courtroom where they had just operated on Mr. Patel. Maazin sighed and ran his hand through his hair.

The panic in him was rising and his shoulder twinged where it had been dislocated the night Ali had died, as it always did when he was about to have a full-on panic attack.

Right now he had to calm himself down.

He felt useless, but if he didn't get his emotions under control he would indeed be useless to everyone.

"Your Highness?"

Maazin spun around, annoyed that he'd been interrupted. Mustafa stood there and Maazin could tell that he was nervous.

"What's wrong? Tell me."

Mustafa handed him a piece of paper. "This came in. There's a storm brewing. Not a cyclone like Blandine, but it's headed straight for Petrie. I've sent my crew out to bring those who are in the tent city here, but I need more help."

Maazin nodded. "I'll come with you. Let's go."

He hurried after Mustafa. Jeena and the first responders who were here could tend to the wounded, but right now he needed to help Mustafa bring in the others. It may not be a cyclone that was headed for Petrie, but a storm hitting an already ravaged island was dangerous enough.

And it appeared that he and Jeena were spending the night here, whether she liked it or not.

They were stuck.

Jeena walked among the cots that had been salvaged, along with the other mattresses and bedding that were scattered across the floor. The displaced and uninjured survivors were put in another courtroom. The little courtroom that they'd used to operate on Mr. Patel earlier in the day had been cleaned.

The storm had struck an hour ago. It was strong and the wind howled fiercely, scaring the small children who had already been through the turmoil of Blandine.

Jeena was exhausted, but she wanted to make sure that everyone was taken care of.

There was a quiet calm, broken only by the odd cough.

All the wounded and sick were stable. Mr. Patel was doing well and Ayesha was staying with him, as was his daughter.

Where did Maazin go?

Jeena had been looking for him since she'd heard that he'd gone out to collect the villagers and bring them to the safety of the courthouse. She'd seen him briefly helping Mustafa board up the windows, but now he was gone.

He was probably hungry and she had a bowl of jasmine rice and vegetable curry that Mustafa's wife was dishing out to everyone.

Maazin had to eat.

She wandered down another hall toward

more offices, and found Maazin in one of them, sitting behind the desk, brooding in the shadows.

She knocked on the door. "I've been looking for you."

"Ah, I just needed a few moments and Mustafa thought that I would be comfortable in here." He rolled his eyes. "Apparently a prince needs a giant room all to himself."

"Do you?" she asked, amused.

"No. I would be more comfortable on my yacht, but my security team, which arrived just after us, advised that this would indeed be a safer location."

"I believe they're right," she said. "I have food. Mustafa's wife is making food for everyone and it's good. Very filling."

"It smells good." Maazin reached over and flicked on a small torch. The generator had been powered down to conserve fuel until the storm was over. Jeena came into the room and set the small metal plate down in front of him, together with a fork.

"Did you eat?" Maazin asked.

"I did. I wouldn't lie and say it was good if it wasn't," she teased, and she sat down in the chair on the opposite side of the desk.

Maazin took a bite. "That is quite wonderful."

"See, I don't lie."

He smiled at her. "How is Mr. Patel doing?"

"He's doing well." That was the truth and Jeena was relieved about that. He had been so close to death. "He's our most critical case and he's stable. Everyone else is in good shape too. For being such a small island with no doctor here, they're doing remarkably well."

"Well, let's hope they do eventually get their own doctor. My father listens to Sara and I'm sure he'll support her ideas."

Jeena snorted. "Right."

Maazin cocked an eyebrow. "My father does a lot of good."

"I know he does, but you can understand my derision, can't you?"

"No. I don't, actually."

"Kalyana is trying to be a modern country. Yet there's nowhere to teach people past high school. Your father has been King for a long time and that change hasn't happened yet."

"He has been King for a long time, but he isn't the ultimate rule-maker. There's parliament and procedures."

"So your father's ideas are not put through? Are you saying he's wanted a university?" she asked in disbelief.

Maazin sighed. "Fine. He can be stubborn and maybe not always think so progressively. He's getting better."

"You do agree with them anyway, don't you?"

Maazin sighed. "Yes."

"Like the marriage thing?" Jeena regretted asking him about it the moment the question left her lips, but she couldn't help it. She didn't understand why Maazin had agreed to marry Lady Meleena if he hadn't loved her. Maazin had always told her that he was against arranged marriage, even though his parents and Ali's arranged marriage had been successful.

He'd always told her that he wanted to marry for love and now he wasn't. It just didn't make sense.

Unless he actually had loved Lady Meleena.

"You weren't forced into it, were you?" Jeena asked, embarrassed that she was assuming that he was an unwilling participant.

"No. I agreed to it."

It stung, even though she didn't want it to sting.

It's because you still care about him. After all this time, you still care deeply for him.

"I'm sorry, then. I didn't mean…" She trailed off, not sure of what to say next, and she stood up to leave. "I'm sorry."

She tried to leave the room, before she continued to put her foot in her mouth. She really didn't know what had come over her, but as she tried to leave she felt a hand on her arm, pulling her back, and she saw Maazin standing behind her.

How had he got to her so fast?

His touch sent a shiver of delight down her spine. And suddenly all she could hear was the sound of her pulse racing in her ears and the rain hammering against the roof.

She forgot everything else as she stared up into those eyes she'd loved so much. The eyes of the man that she'd loved so much, the man who haunted her dreams.

She looked away. It was too much.

"Jeena, it's not like that. I agreed to it because it made diplomatic sense, because it's my duty. That's it. I didn't love her."

Jeena looked up stunned. "You didn't?"

"No."

"Didn't you care for her at least? I mean, you agreed to marry her."

"Because it was my duty but, no, I didn't care for her because she wasn't you," he whispered. He took a step closer to her and touched her face, like he had all those years ago on Patang Island.

Her heart skipped a beat and her body shook, craving more of his touch. And then, before she knew what was happening, his hands were in her hair and he was pulling her close, kissing her, and she let him.

She let him kiss her, very gently, and her body began to melt, powerless.

There was a knock at the door and Jeena jumped back, embarrassed by what she'd let happen.

"Jeena…" Maazin pleaded.

She shook her head. "No. I'm not falling into that trap again."

"I'm not engaged," Maazin said.

"It doesn't matter. This can't happen."

"Why?" he asked.

But before she could say anything further, before she fell into the trap of believing and trusting him again, she opened the door to find Ayesha there.

"Dr. Harrak, it's Mr. Patel. His temperature has spiked again."

"I'll be right there."

Ayesha nodded and left.

Jeena took a calming breath and looked back at Maazin. It was too late for them. Even if he was no longer engaged to Meleena, he was off limits. She couldn't be with him again, she was too afraid of being hurt, and when this was all over she was going back to Canada, back to her son, and would try to put this whole thing behind her.

CHAPTER SEVEN

THE STORM BLEW itself out overnight, although there was a storm raging inside him. He knew he shouldn't have kissed her, but he'd been unable to prevent it.

And even though no one else was supposed to know that his engagement to Lady Meleena was over, he'd wanted Jeena to know. And he was glad he'd told her. He was just angry with himself for kissing her.

What had he been thinking?

At least no one had seen them. Jeena may know his engagement was off, but the rest of the world didn't.

His parents would be furious if the announcement was made now. Hadn't he done enough damage to his family?

Still, he'd been unable to help himself. When he was around her she made him feel alive again.

Maazin tossed and turned all night, guilt eating away at him.

He was so selfish.

In the morning Maazin went out with Mustafa to survey the damage, which was minimal thankfully. The last thing Petrie Island needed was to have more of the small island torn apart.

Still it was clear to Maazin that Petrie needed more help than he and Jeena could offer. It would take a long time to repair the damage that Blandine had done. Thankfully not many lives had been lost.

Maazin got on the satellite phone in his yacht and called Farhan for assistance, and Farhan promised he would send more manpower and supplies needed to rebuild Petrie.

It only took about five hours for shelters, food and water, to arrive, as well as a relief physician who was a young doctor from Kalyana, which mean that he and Jeena could leave.

Her time was almost up. Farhan told Maazin that Jeena had been called back to Canada now that Kalyana was getting back on its feet. She would be leaving soon.

The thought of Jeena having to leave

again struck him with a sense of dread that he wasn't prepared for. The official date hadn't been given by the Canadian consulate, but Jeena's time in Kalyana was coming to an end and he didn't like it one bit.

You should be relieved.

He should be happy to have this closure. He now knew what had happened to Jeena all those years ago so he would never have to wonder about that again. It had given him the closure he needed so he could move forward.

Really?

No, he didn't really believe that, because he knew deep down that he would never be *over* Jeena and that kiss they'd shared last night just proved how much he still wanted her. Even after all this time when he'd thought she'd betrayed him and left him.

When he'd realized Jeena had left he hadn't cared about anything. And that lack of care had cost Ali his life and eventually set Maazin on the path to right his wrongs and save others by serving his country.

His dedication and passion for that had driven Meleena away and disappointed his parents yet again, but he didn't care that Meleena had left.

He'd never loved her.

He didn't even like her.

It was Jeena. Always Jeena.

He still wanted her. Wanted no other, it was just that he couldn't have her. He didn't deserve to have her.

And it was clear that Jeena no longer wanted him. She no longer wanted a life in Kalyana when Canada offered so much more for her. It was for the best.

And he wouldn't subject Jeena to this life of protocol, this shackle of being a member of the royal family.

He wouldn't do that to his son.

His son. As much as he didn't want this life for Syman, he wanted to be a part of Syman's life. Why did it have to be so complicated?

Perhaps it doesn't?

Maazin finished loading the yacht with the supplies the islanders didn't need and then saw Jeena coming toward him with her duffel bag on her back and carrying the bio-hazard container with her surgical instruments.

The duffel bag looked larger than her and he didn't know how she was carrying it all so easily. He met her down on the pier and held out his hand.

"What?" Jeena asked.

"Let me carry that for you."

"I can carry it. I'm used to carrying it."

"That must be heavy," Maazin remarked.

"I can deadlift over a eighty-five with ease and back-squat with the same. I think I can handle this."

He raised his eyebrows. "What?"

Jeena chuckled. "You think you're the only one who works out? I do strength training. I have to be able to manage out in the field on my own or with very little help. Who else is going to carry my gear?"

Maazin was impressed and he took the biohazard bucket. "Let me at least make sure this secure so we don't have a mess. The ocean is a bit choppy after the storm."

"Deal."

Maazin helped her on board and they secured everything and then cast off from Petrie Island, heading back south toward the main island.

Jeena sat beside him on the bridge and that tension that always seemed to be there settled in again. He hated that. Talking to her had once been so easy, but he'd been a different person then.

He'd felt more free. He hadn't necessarily been free, but he'd felt more free. Of course, that relaxed disposition had caused nothing but trouble. It had caused nothing but a world of hurt and pain that he was never going to be able to make up to anyone.

Not to his parents.

Not to Farhan.

Not to Jeena.

And not to himself.

He deserved his sentence. He deserved the unhappiness, and the best he could do was try and take care of his people.

"I want to thank you again for the work you did on Petrie," Maazin said, breaking the silence.

"You're welcome. That's why I'm here."

"Would you have come back had it not been for the cyclone?" Even though he knew the answer to that.

Jeena's expression was sad. "No. I didn't want him growing up here as an illegitimate lovechild."

Maazin flinched at her harsh words. "I am sorry. I wouldn't have let that happen."

Jeena shrugged. "I did what was best for

myself and for Syman. My parents chose to give up everything to come with me. I can never repay them enough. They didn't have to come with me, but if they hadn't given up so much to support me, I wouldn't be a surgeon now."

"I am sorry. Your family shouldn't have had to give up so much just because of who I am."

Tears welled up in her eyes and she looked away. "Thank you."

"I have received word from the consulate that your orders have been changed and you will be called back to Canada in a matter of days."

Jeena brushed away her tears. "What?"

"Kalyana is getting back on its feet and Canada has called back its special services. Not to sound too clichéd, but the British are coming."

"That doesn't make sense." She checked her phone and frowned. "You're right, my orders have arrived. In five days we'll be heading back to Canada."

"You'll be able to see Syman again," Maazin said gently. He was trying to give her something to be happy about because maybe if she was happy then he would feel happy too. Right now, he didn't feel happy about it.

Though it was for the best that she leave.

"Patang Island," Maazin remarked. "It looks so peaceful now."

Jeena nodded. "I wanted to go back. I wanted to visit all my old haunts before I left again, because it would probably be the last time I saw them."

"Well, let's go, then," he offered.

"What?" Jeena asked, confused. "We can't go to Patang Island."

"Why not?" Maazin asked, turning the wheel to head his yacht around to the lee side of the island, where they would be safe and wouldn't come up on a reef. From there they could take the small dinghy out to the sandbar and he could give her a short time of peace.

Later, he would take her back to her family's old home. He owned the plantation now and kept up the vanilla production. Jeena's old family home was used as a small bed and breakfast establishment now, but was currently empty because no tourists had been allowed to come to Kalyana since Blandine had hit, and any tourists that had been in Kalyana had been evacuated.

Not that many tourists took the long trip to Kalyana.

The Seychelles were much more popular, and didn't have quite the pomp and circumstance that Kalyana and his father demanded.

"Maazin, this is crazy," Jeena shouted above the wind as he sped toward the island. "Your security team will go bananas when you don't pass their certain check points in time."

"So let them. We're safe. Kalyana's waters are monitored. Let's just take this moment. You wanted to go back to Patang Island and we shall."

Jeena smiled. "Okay."

He came up on the lee side of the island and anchored in a safe spot where they wouldn't run aground from shifting tides but were safe from the waves or any surges.

"Why don't you change out of your uniform? There may be some women's clothing in the main berth. Farhan and Sara sometimes take the yacht out."

"That sounds good." Jeena disappeared below deck and Maazin let out a sigh as he listened to the gentle waves in the shelter of the island and the large reef that surrounded it lap against the side of his boat.

What're you doing?

He didn't know. He just wanted to give this to her. He just wanted to spend this time with her. When she left this time he didn't want her to leave and think about him or this country with bad thoughts.

And when Syman asked about him, if he did, then he would know that he was always welcome in Kalyana.

"Are you okay?"

Maazin turned around and took a step back when he saw Jeena in an emerald-green sari. It was the same color as the dress she had been wearing that first time he'd seen her. It took him right back to that moment.

And his breath was literally taken away.

"You look beautiful," he murmured.

A flush of pink rose in her cheeks. "Thank you."

"You ready?" he asked.

"Yes," she said nervously. "I think I am."

He smiled and took her hand. He climbed over the side first and down the ladder into the dinghy. She followed and he helped her, slipping his hands around her waist and guiding her safely down. It made his pulse quicken and the urge to kiss her, like he'd done last night, overtook him, but he held back.

He didn't want to scare her off.

This time on the island was to give her another memory of her homeland. It was something for her to cherish before she left again, and he wanted her to have that untainted.

He didn't want to make it any more awkward than it was between them. All he wanted at this moment was to give her a good memory. It was the least he could give her, especially when he'd missed so much.

He guided the little motored dinghy to the sandbar and cut the motor when he got close. He leaped over the side into the cool water and pulled the dinghy ashore.

Jeena stood up and without thinking he just lifted her up, gripping her waist and setting her down on the shore. She gasped when he set her down and he stared into her dark, warm eyes, lost for a moment.

"Maazin," she whispered.

"Yes."

"You can let go of me."

"Right," he said quickly. "Of course."

She blushed and took his hands in hers.

Her hands were so tiny, so soft. "Come on, let's enjoy this moment of peace."

"Good idea."

Only she didn't let go of his hand and he didn't pull it away. He liked holding her hand as they walked barefoot on the sand. It was windy, but he didn't care. It was beautiful out here. The ocean and whitecaps. The sun reflecting against the water and causing it to sparkle. The sand seemed to shimmer like diamonds. They walked over to the lone piece of driftwood that Maazin had hauled up out of the water ten years ago. It was a place to sit.

"I can't believe that it's still here," Jeena said wistfully.

"Well, it was quite large, but I'm surprised it hasn't rotted away to nothing."

Jeena smiled and let go of his hand to run her hand along the rough wood. "I'm glad it's still here. That night…"

"The night we conceived Syman."

A blush tinged her cheek. "Yes."

"That was a magical night for me too. I'm sorry that I missed his birth, I'm sorry that I wasn't there for it all."

She nodded and sat down on the log. "Me too."

"Does he ask about me?" It was a question he'd been avoiding and he was afraid of asking it, but he had to know. It was eating him up not to ask.

"He does," Jeena said quietly, looking at her hands.

"What have you told him about me?"

"I told him you lived in Kalyana and I told him that I had lost touch with you, but that if you knew about him, you would love him."

Maazin nodded and sat down next to her. "That is true."

He wanted to tell her that if he had known it would all have been different, but he wasn't sure about that. He knew one thing—he was sad that this life with Jeena and his son had been taken from him. That he'd never got the chance to ask her to be his. He'd never seen his son as a baby. Never held him in his arms. He'd missed so much.

And you are responsible for taking Ali's life.

That thought grounded him. He didn't deserve it. Ali had never got a chance and he didn't deserve it either. It was fitting justice for his sins.

"Tell me about his birth. Tell me about Syman's birth."

Jeena looked at him like he was crazy. "What?"

"Tell me. When was he born?"

"June twenty-sixth. It was a Friday and he was born in the morning. He came out screaming and had all this dark hair, even on his bottom." She chuckled about that. "I thought he was going to be made fun of for being so hairy, but it was just lanugo and it fell out as he got older. Then he was this chubby, happy baby who slept all night in a bassinet by my bedside. Everyone who saw him loved him."

It cut him to the quick to hear about this. He'd been denied that precious time. He hadn't had a chance to hold him in his arms, to kiss his head and sing him to sleep.

"It must've been hard on you, getting a medical degree and having an infant."

"It was. My mother and father were my lifeline. If I didn't have them, I wouldn't be a doctor. They knew how much I wanted to be a doctor when we still lived in Kalyana and before I met you they were saving up all they could to send me to England or Australia to get my education, but then I attended that polo match and met you."

Maazin touched her face. "I'm sorry that I ruined your life."

Jeena touched his hand, still cupping her face. "You didn't ruin my life, Maazin. You gave me this great gift. Syman is a wonderful boy and my life in Canada is good. Do I wish that things could have been different and that I'd chosen my life in Canada myself, instead of it being thrust on me, yes, but my parents are better off there than they were here. We have a good life. Don't feel bad."

"You are too kind. Kinder than I deserve."

"What're you talking about?"

Maazin sighed. "I am the one who killed Ali."

Her eyes widened. "What're you talking about?"

"I'm telling you the truth. I am the one who killed Ali. It was my fault."

It took Jeena a moment to let the words sink in. What did Maazin mean that he was the one responsible for killing Ali?

"I thought it was a car accident?" she asked.

Maazin stood and was pacing on the sand, rubbing the back of his neck. "It was."

"Were you driving?" she asked.

"No."

"Then I don't quite understand how you're responsible for your brother's death."

"I was drunk. I had gone to a party that I shouldn't have been at. There was drinking and some drugs. I didn't do the drugs, but I was very drunk and I couldn't call security to come and get me. I was already splashed across the tabloids and when I called the palace, drunk again, Ali took it upon himself to come and get me. His wife came with him." Maazin closed his eyes and she could tell that it was hard for him to continue.

"Go on," Jeena urged gently. "What happened?"

"Ali came, of course. He was such a good brother." Maazin took a deep breath. "He came and got me. Both of them scolded me, of course, for being blind drunk and at a party I should not have gone to. Not that I did anything, I just got drunk with my friends. The house was up in the hills and while we were driving home a rainstorm hit. It rained very hard, or so they tell me, I don't remember. What I remember is Ali yelling at me, telling me that I had to pull up my socks and behave better.

"Then there was this loud bang and screaming and we were upside down, before it went black. I woke up in agony because my shoulder was dislocated and I was under the wrecked car. Ali and Chandni were dead."

Jeena gasped and she could see the pain in Maazin's eyes as he poured out his story to her. It was obvious that it weighed heavily on him and that it had been traumatic.

"Maazin, you were not responsible for your brother's death."

"Of course I was!" he snapped. "If he hadn't been such a good brother he would've sent someone to come and get me. But he didn't. He came himself because I begged him not to tell Father. I was terrified or... I really don't know. I don't remember much about the phone call. Only that I wanted Ali to come and get me. And if I hadn't been so insistent and he hadn't been such a good brother he would still be alive. And so would Chandni.

"It wasn't just his life I ruined. I ruined my parents' lives. Ali was my father's favorite. And then I ruined my late sister-in-law's parents' lives. They lost their daughter. And then Farhan was made Crown Prince. He had to come back from Australia and give up his life there…"

Jeena stood and walked over to him, and reached up and touched his face. "It's not your fault. Ali loved you, but it's not your fault that he and his wife chose to come get you that night. You are not to be blamed."

"Lady Meleena blames me for the end of our farce of an engagement."

Jeena's heart skipped a beat. "Oh?"

It shouldn't matter to her that his engagement was over. She shouldn't care, but she did.

"When Ali died I devoted my life to saving others and my duties. They took all my attention."

"Is that why the engagement went on for so long?"

He nodded. "Partly, but mostly I didn't care about her. There was only one person I cared about."

"I cared about you too," she said softly. She truly had never stopped caring about him.

There had been no one else.

Don't fall for him again. Don't do it.

He took a step closer to her. Those gray-green eyes twinkled as he caressed her face.

Her body trembled like a traitor to her own mind under his touch.

And before she knew what was happening he wrapped his arms around her and kissed her, just like before, and she was lost to him. Her body wanted more.

She hadn't been able to stop thinking about that kiss that had snuck up on them in the office on Petrie. She wanted to forget that kiss because she was leaving and nothing could happen between them, even if that pull of attraction and feelings was still there.

It was off limits.

She couldn't give everything up for a chance with him. She didn't come from his world any more. She didn't want that kind of spotlight on her or Syman.

And as much as she wanted this kiss to continue, she knew that it couldn't. She couldn't let it continue so she pushed on his chest to move him away from her.

"We can't," she whispered, trying to calm the erratic beat of her pulse and quell the fire that was in her blood. "We can't."

"Why not?" he whispered, leaning his forehead down to hers. Their foreheads were pressed together, their arms around each other.

"You need someone to be your wife and I am not that woman. I can never be that woman."

Maazin nodded. "I understand. I'm sorry for kissing you. It's just that around you, I lose myself. It feels like all those years ago."

"I know, but it's not." She tried not to let the tears stinging her eyes spill down her cheeks. She wanted to tell him that she wanted to be his and that she'd never got over him, but that was selfish. Syman had a life in Canada. He had friends and loved his school, his hockey and his home.

Her parents had given up so much so that they could go with her and help her. Now they were prosperous and she couldn't ask them to give it all up to chase a whim.

Her mother had tried to warn her all those years ago that getting involved with Maazin was a bad idea, but she had been young and foolish then…

"You shouldn't get involved with the Prince," her mother said quietly. "Nothing good can come from that."

"What do you mean? He loves me. I know he does."

Her mother took her hands. "I have no doubt. Who could not love you? You are beautiful. But you are just a farmer's daughter and he is a prince."

"But Kalyana is a free country and he's the third son."

"Jeena, please be careful. I don't want you to get hurt..."

She should've listened to her mother back then. If she had she wouldn't have fallen in love with a man who was off limits. A man who had ruined her for all others. But she had been young and so foolish.

She wasn't going to make that mistake again. When she'd been sent to Kalyana, she'd promised herself that she wouldn't let herself be sucked in again.

She had to remind herself of that.

"We should go," she said, stepping away from him. It was safer to put some distance between the two of them.

Maazin nodded.

Jeena turned and walked back to the dinghy. There was a cool wind and it caused a shiver to run through her. The sun disappeared behind a cloud and suddenly things didn't seem so rosy and lovely on Patang Island.

It had lost its sparkle and magic.

It just reminded her of a life with a person she loved that she could never have. The best thing she could do now was walk away and try to just forget about Kalyana and Maazin's kisses, even if she knew that was going to be a hard, hard thing to do.

An impossible thing to do, but it was for the best.

CHAPTER EIGHT

THE MOMENT THAT Maazin docked in the harbor, there were several limousines waiting, as well as his brother's personnel. He had a bad feeling about what he was seeing.

He glanced over at Jeena, who had changed back into her medical uniform. She bit her lip, worrying about it, and he could see the fear in her eyes.

"Don't worry," he said. "They're here for me."

"Don't be so sure. We did take a detour and I am not Lady Meleena. Remember the world thinks you're still engaged to her."

"That I am aware of," he said quickly. "No one else knows about you, Jeena, and no one else knows about my broken engagement. You are a doctor, a Canadian doctor. It's all proper."

"If you say so." She didn't sound too convinced. She tried to walk past him, but he held her back.

"I won't let anyone hurt you," he said, and he meant it.

"Thanks," she whispered.

The moment Maazin's yacht was tied up and he helped Jeena down onto the pier, Farhan, flanked by two bodyguards, came quickly toward them. He was frowning and there were dark circles under his eyes.

A shiver ran down his spine.

Oh, God.

"Farhan?" Maazin asked, barely getting the words out.

"Maazin, it's Father. He took a spell this morning and we've been waiting for your return." Farhan glanced over at Jeena. "Are you Dr. Harrak?"

"Yes," she said nervously.

"Oh, good. We were looking for you. Your team said that you were able to perform a catheterization under less than ideal circumstances and that you were the best."

"I… I am, but…" Jeena was stumbling over her words and Maazin knew it was because of who his father was. His father was the King. She was terrified of operating on the King.

He knew what she was thinking. She

thought she already had a bad reputation with the Kalyanese people.

"Jeena, nothing bad will happen to you at the palace, not while you are under my care."

Jeena looked at him and nodded. "Of course. Of course I can help His Majesty."

Farhan cocked an eyebrow. He was confused, but he wasn't about to argue about reasons now out on the public pier at the harbor. "Well, the royal motorcade will take you both to the palace."

Maazin put his hand on the small of Jeena's back and urged her to take a step forward. A bodyguard stepped forward and took her duffel bag from her.

Another took her surgical kit. Maazin stuck by her side as they were ushered into a limo where Farhan was already seated. Jeena chewed on her lip again and began to wring her hands.

Maazin wanted to reach out and comfort her, but Farhan was watching her with interest.

"Dr. Harrak, are you quite all right?" Farhan asked.

"Fine. It's just, I've never operated on royalty before. Never done a cardiac cath procedure on a king!"

Farhan smiled. "It'll be okay, I assure you.

We have everything you need. I would do it myself, but I can't, as you know, being his son. So even Sara is unable to operate. It's driving her a bit mad, because she wants to help."

Jeena chuckled, but Maazin could still hear the nervousness in her voice.

"It'll be quite all right. You are a capable surgeon. You did an appendectomy in a courthouse and Mr. Patel is going to make a full recovery because of it, and you taught a first responder the ins and outs of being a scrub nurse. You are capable of this. Do not think about who he is, just think of him as any other patient."

Maazin's words were meant to calm her.
"Think of him as any other patient."
Which was easier said than done, but she was going to try. She had to try. They approached the palace and passed through Huban's gate and up to the palace. It sat on top of a hill and reflected the rich history of Kalyana's Eastern influence. It was like a fortress, but surrounded with lush, green vegetation. Or at least it had been, but when cyclone Blandine had blown through, the leaves had been stripped away and trees toppled. As they came closer to the pal-

ace she could see gardeners trying to clean up the mess that Blandine had left in her wake. The drive was littered with brightly colored petals that had been trampled down and crushed into the road.

It was sad.

The palace with its warm-hued stone walls and arched windows had been the center of Huban. It had been the heart of Kalyana and now it looked the worse for wear. As if Kalyana's heart had been broken.

At least her spirit hadn't been broken. Of that Jeena was sure.

The limo pulled up in front of two, large ornately carved doors that were immediately opened. Farhan slid out and Maazin followed, but Jeena felt frozen.

"Jeena?" Maazin asked. "Are you coming?"

"Yes."

She could do this. She'd sworn an oath as a doctor to do no harm and she was going to stick to that oath. She was not going to put her medical career in jeopardy because she was worried about operating on the Kalyanese King. And she wasn't going to embarrass her new country by being the Canadian doctor who couldn't save the life of the Kalyanese King.

Forget that!

She was going to save his life. For as much as she was nervous about operating on King Uttam, she loved Maazin and she knew that Maazin cared about his father. Even if he seemed to blame himself for Ali's death.

Maazin held out his hand, which was breaking protocol, and she smiled at him. She reached out and took his hand as he helped her out of the limousine. His hand was strong and he believed in her. She was going to do this for him.

Once she was out of the limo, he let go of her hand and she took another deep breath, calming her nerves.

Here we go. You've got this.

She straightened her shoulders and held her head high as she followed Farhan and Maazin through the large double doors into an entranceway of white marble and creamy stone walls that gleamed brightly.

"Maazin, so you've finally decided to grace us with your presence."

Jeena glanced up to see Queen Aruna standing there, regal and poised. She didn't smile and she didn't seem to look worried or have any kind of emotion as she looked at her sons.

Maazin walked over to his mother and took her hand in his, bowing over it.

"I'm sorry, Mother," Maazin apologized. "I was only doing my duty to my people."

"Yes. That's all very well and good, but we had to send Farhan out to fetch you. Your yacht was late getting in."

Jeena could sense the tension, the coldness and the detachment between Queen Aruna and Maazin. It was like they were strangers rather than mother and son. Perhaps Aruna did blame Maazin for Ali's death. There was a huge rift between them.

It was sad.

She was so close to Syman. She could never treat Syman with such aloofness.

"I'm sorry, Mother." Maazin stepped back and the Queen's hardened gaze fell on her.

Jeena curtseyed. "Your Majesty."

"Dr. Harrak, I am so glad you've come and I understand from my daughter-in-law that you're also Kalyanese."

Queen Aruna addressed her very politely, but Jeena could hear the undercurrent of displeasure and Jeena realized then Queen Aruna knew *exactly* who she was.

"Yes, Your Majesty." Jeena straightened. "How can I be of assistance?"

"Farhan, you're a doctor—please explain

it to our dear doctor and then take her to your father to perform the procedure. Please excuse me, but I haven't slept in the last twenty-four hours." Queen Aruna excused herself. She turned back up the stairs and disappeared out of sight.

Farhan turned to her. "Dr. Harrak, my father has a pulmonary embolus and he needs catheterization to remove it before it does further damage. My father has had a stroke in the past and he suffers from macular degeneration as well as atrial fibrillation."

"And none of your surgeons can perform it?" Jeena asked.

"Not under these conditions. In a hospital, yes, but we were told by your team that you were able to do it and you had done it successfully before." Farhan looked over at Maazin. "Again, none of us in the royal family can assist you, but there are some of the finest royal physicians in attendance. He is prepped and waiting for the procedure. He's had a sedative and is groggy."

Jeena nodded. "Take me to him."

Farhan bowed his head and gestured to show her the way. She was led down a hallway to a small antechamber and a room that was used a formal sitting room for visiting dignitaries. Only now it had been transformed into a procedure room.

Jeena glanced through the window and saw that King Uttam was laid out and prepped. They were just waiting for her.

You've got this. This is just another patient. He's not a king. He's a human being who needs your help. He's not your King right now. He's a patient. Just an ordinary, normal patient.

"There are scrubs in this room here and a place to scrub in," Farhan offered. "I'll leave you to it. Maazin, if you'll follow me."

"Just one moment," Maazin said. He took a step toward her and his presence was reassuring. She wished that he could stay with her. She wanted him to stay, she needed him there while she did this procedure on the King of her homeland.

She didn't want to be known as the doctor who killed the King of Kalyana.

"You can do this," Maazin whispered.

"I'm frightened," she whispered back. "This is your father...the King."

"He's just a patient. This is like any other patient you'd work on and try to save. You can do this." He took a step back and turned away with his brother.

Jeena took another deep breath and then

went to get changed. She quickly changed into the scrubs that had been left for her, cleaned herself up and then headed into the makeshift procedure room.

Another doctor was there.

"Dr. Harrak, I'm Dr. Imran Patel, and I'll be your assist."

Jeena nodded. "It's a pleasure to meet you."

Jeena walked over to the King and looked down at him. He was mostly out of it, but not completely under. The King's gaze locked on to her and he smiled, as if she was an old friend and not some commoner who'd had his secret illegitimate grandchild. He probably didn't even know about Syman. Which was for the best.

"You look familiar," the King whispered.

"My name is Dr. Harrak. Jeena Harrak. I'm from Canada, previously from Kalyana."

The King's eyes widened. "I've heard of you. You have a son, don't you? A son who plays hockey."

Jeena's heart dropped to the soles of her feet and she felt faint. How did he know about Syman? How did he know that Syman played hockey? And then she realized that Kalyana had been keeping tabs on her for some time, even from as far away as Canada. She had been a fool to think otherwise.

It rattled her completely.

She wanted to turn and run. She wanted to run back to Canada and hide Syman, but she couldn't do that. She couldn't turn her back on a patient who needed her services, even if she felt like that patient posed a threat to her family.

She would save King Uttam's life and if he came for Syman, she would remind him how she'd saved his life and perhaps he would feel he owed her a debt and that debt would protect her son from this life of protocol and pomp.

Maazin was worried about Jeena. She looked so nervous, doing the procedure on his father, and he couldn't blame her one bit. If the situation had been reversed he would feel the same way. He couldn't stop pacing as he waited with Farhan in their father's office.

Maazin knew that his constant pacing was antagonizing his father's macaw Sophie, because she would squawk every so often when he got close to her perch.

"You're driving that bird crazy with your incessant pacing," Farhan remarked calmly. "Truth be told, you're driving me crazy too."

"I can't help it. I'm worried about her."
And then he pinched the bridge of his nose
and cursed inwardly for the slip.

"Are you having an affair with the Canadian doctor?"

"What're you talking about?" Maazin
asked, trying to keep calm.

Farhan rolled his eyes. "I see the way you
look at her. Be careful. The public thinks
you are still with Lady Meleena."

"I'm not!" Maazin snapped. He was annoyed with his brother's questions.

"Having an affair?"

"I am not with Lady Meleena and not having an affair with Dr. Harrak. At least..."

"At least what?" Farhan asked cautiously.
"You're not having an affair with Dr. Harrak,
are you? Please tell me you're not."

"No, but... I did."

"When?" Farhan asked, confused. "You've
been nothing but faithful to Lady Meleena.
Even when you two were apart for so long."

"And look where that got me. She had her
own countless affairs."

"I'm sorry she hurt you," Farhan said.

Maazin ran his hand through his hair.
"Meleena did hurt me. But I couldn't care
less about her and the men she saw. It was
something else."

"Really?" Farhan asked.

"I never wanted to marry Lady Meleena."

Farhan rolled his eyes as if to say, *I know that*. "You promised Father."

"So?"

"I married who Father told me to marry."

"And I'm glad it worked out for you and I'm glad it worked out for Ali too and our parents. I'm glad for every arranged marriage that works out, but…" He scrubbed his hands over his face. "Ten years ago, before Ali died, I was in love with someone else and that's Jeena. I adored her, worshipped her and I wanted only her. Then she vanished. Mother told me she'd left and there was a letter Meleena found. I was distraught and hurt. Little did I know that Jeena left because she was pregnant and she was afraid of having the illegitimate child of a prince."

Farhan's eyes widened. "She was pregnant and Meleena knew? It all seems very odd."

"I know."

"Should we let Jeena be operating on Father, then?" Farhan asked with a frown, getting to his feet. "She's the mother of your child."

"She won't harm him. She takes her oath seriously. She came to Kalyana because of her love and respect for Canada and Kalyana. She is the last person to do him harm."

"How did you find out about...your child?"

Maazin nodded. "Syman. I have a son. A son I've never met and his name is Syman. He's nine."

"Why didn't she tell you about him? Even if she left for Canada with her parents she could've called or mailed a letter, even gone to the tabloids."

"She wanted to protect her son and Meleena told her that I didn't want our child. That I didn't want her."

"And clearly you did."

"Yes."

Farhan ran his hand through his hair. "And yet Father arranged for you to marry Meleena, who manipulated all this? If Father had known about his grandchiid, he would have insisted you marry Jeena. Father loves his children."

"He loved Ali," Maazin said bitterly, and then his shoulders slumped. He hated bringing Ali up.

"When are you going to stop blaming yourself for that?" Farhan asked.

Maazin didn't answer him. Instead he looked back at the portrait of their father that hung on the wall. Next to it was a portrait of Ali.

Ali had been his parents' favorite.

And Maazin had destroyed that. His mother had made that all too clear to him.

I'm sorry, Aii. So sorry.

"Well, that explains her nervousness," Farhan said, breaking the silence that had descended between the two of them. "I thought it just had something to do with operating on the King."

"Well, I'm sure that's part of it," Maazin said.

"What're you going to do about your son?"

"I promised Jeena that I wouldn't hurt her and it would hurt her if I tried to claim him and bring him into this life. I don't want to do that to him."

"He has a right to know who his father is," Farhan stated. "He has a right to know where he comes from."

Maazin sighed. "I know, but…"

Do I really want him to know? Do I deserve to have him in my life?

He left Farhan standing there and walked out onto the terrace. He didn't want to talk about it any more. He didn't want to dwell on the things he couldn't have. He'd hurt Jeena just as deeply as she'd hurt him.

There was no going back. Even if he desperately wanted to.

She'd made it clear that there was no going back for her.

Jeena pulled off her surgical mask and then walked out of the room. The King had tolerated the procedure well and she'd removed the clot. He was being moved to his own bed to recover.

Jeena slid down the wall and tried to take a few calming breaths.

She'd saved King Uttam's life, but he knew about her son.

He hadn't actually acknowledged that Syman was Maazin's but he knew about her son. How did he know about him?

She wanted to call her parents about it and ask their advice, but she didn't want to send them into a tizzy.

Jeena closed her eyes and tried to find her center, a place that had always calmed her. That place was standing out on her bedroom balcony overlooking the green lush hills, the fields of vanilla, and beyond all that she was tall enough to see the ocean.

How she wished she could go back there.

Even for a moment.

"How did it go?"

Jeena opened her eyes to see Maazin standing in the shadows.

"Are you supposed to be here?"

"Father's been moved. I'm allowed to be here." He smiled. "Are you all right?"

"No. That was… It was hard and I feel dizzy. I wish I could reach out to my parents and talk to them about it, but I don't want to worry them. That's the last thing I want to do, so I was trying to find my happy place."

"And where is that?" Maazin asked.

"My old home. The plantation."

"Then let's go," he offered.

"Shouldn't you be here or with your father?"

"It won't matter I'm gone. He won't care."

Jeena tilted her head to the side. She could see the pain in his eyes, the blame he bore. "Are you so sure?"

"Do you want to go or not?" he asked.

"I do, but my family doesn't own it any longer."

"I know," Maazin stated. "I went there after you left. I thought maybe your parents would be there and I could ask them where you'd gone. I saw that they had left too and the plantation was for sale, so I bought it."

Jeena's eyes widened and she couldn't believe what she was hearing. "You bought it?"

"Yes. I own it. It's still a plantation and during tourist season I rent it out as a little cottage. It's empty at the moment. There are no tourists in Kalyana. We can go there."

Even though she knew she shouldn't go with him, she wanted to go back home. Just for a moment, even if it was with him.

A man who made her lose all control.

A man she couldn't have but still cared for. A man who still owned her heart, even if she didn't want him to.

"Yes! Please."

Maazin nodded. "Go and change and we'll sneak out of the palace and head over there."

Jeena nodded and got up. She hurried off to get changed. She was shocked that Maazin had bought it. It had been his money that had allowed her parents to start a new life in Canada and she'd had no idea.

Why would he buy it?

She shook that thought out of her head, because all she cared about right now was that she got to go home. Even for a brief moment.

She was going home.

CHAPTER NINE

THE CLOSER THEY go to her home, the more excited and emotional Jeena got. She recognized the road they turned down, although it was a better quality road than she remembered. She closed her eyes and thought about all the times she had come down this road on her way home.

There had been some changes, but the scent of the fields and the sight of the orchids that she knew so well hit her, and a tear slid down her face.

Her father had liked to grow his vanilla orchids on wooden poles, as originally orchid vines had grown up trees and her father had always believed that the wood added to the productivity of the fruit.

And he had spent hours and hours checking on the flowers.

He had loved his plantation. He had known everything about it and he'd given it all up for her. She was still in shock that Maazin had bought the plantation. Why had he done that?

As they rounded a bend she cried out as she saw the fields. The vines were still growing on wooden poles. Some were old still and there were also fresh ones, but the fields were neat and tidy, just like she remembered.

She wiped away the tears as she drank in the sight.

"Can you stop the car?" she asked Maazin.

"Of course." Maazin pulled over to the side of the road and Jeena slipped out. She walked up to the fence and climbed up. Teetering precariously, she took a picture for her father. He was sleeping now, so she would send it to him later so it would be the first thing he saw when he woke up.

"We tried to keep it the same," Maazin said, coming up behind her. "Your father knew his stuff and he was admired around these parts. So I made sure that the man who farms this land now does it the way your family has always done it."

Jeena nodded, fighting back tears. "I still can't believe you bought it. Why did you buy it?"

Maazin shrugged. "I didn't want to see it ruined. You loved this place and I didn't understand why your family left. I know why now, but at the time I thought that maybe you would come back and I wanted it here, waiting for you."

"Thank you." She brushed away tears again. "Let's see the house. Please."

"Of course."

They climbed back into the Jeep. Jeena was swallowing back all the emotion that was welling up inside her. She drank in the sights. This was her happy place. This was the place she always came back to in her mind when she was scared, when she was hurt and when she was uncertain.

This was home.

And it was her fault that her family was no longer here.

Maazin pulled into the driveway.

And Jeena cried silent tears as she looked up at the house. The vines still grew on the outside. They weren't vanilla orchids, just plain orchids that her mother loved. The stone path was the same and there was the swing on the big old banyan tree that was said to have grown up through an original post of the first home that had been built when her ancestors had first come here from India in the seventeenth century.

It was all the same. Untouched.

Except it really wasn't the same. Her family wasn't here. It was her home, but the heart of it was gone. It seemed so lonely. So cold.

"Shall we go inside?" Maazin asked softly.

"Yes."

Maazin unlocked the door and stood back, letting her go in first. There were some changes, mostly modernizing to accommodate tourists, but the layout was still the same. Jeena closed her eyes and swore that she could hear her father singing as he came home from a long day in the fields.

She could smell her mother's cooking on the stove. The aroma of her saffron rice wafting in the air. And then the memory of her family frantically packing all their belongings, their sadness as they'd left this house for the very last time.

Jeena climbed the stairs to the room at the top that had been hers. It was no longer her childhood room, but had been converted into a loft space with a gorgeous balcony. A romantic getaway for lovers overlooking the vanilla fields. She opened the balcony doors and walked outside. The sun was setting in the west.

Shades of red and orange reflected off the blue water that lay beyond the rolling green hills filled with flowering vanilla. She could see the path to the creek where she'd almost drowned. And then she saw it, the palace in the distance. She'd forgotten that she would be able to see it from up here. When she'd been a child she'd dreamed of being a princess and wondering what it was like to live in such a palace.

Now she knew and she didn't want that.

Don't you? If you had it you could have Maazin.

It was all too surreal. She wrapped her arms around herself, hugging herself because she was overwhelmed. She'd never thought that she would be back here, that she would be able to see her childhood home again.

"I did make this change to your room. I'm sorry," Maazin said from the door, interrupting her thoughts.

"It's okay," she said, glancing back at him. "You've done a beautiful job and I'm thankful you kept so much the same."

He stood behind her. "I didn't want to change anything too much. I so wanted you to come back."

She looked up at him and her heart began to beat faster. "I wanted to come back too."

He touched her cheek, brushing his thumb

across her skin. "I cared for you, Jeena. I still do."

"Maazin, don't say that."

"I can't help it, Jeena."

"Maazin, I... I cared for you too." A tear slid down her cheek. And it was true. She did.

I still love you.

Only she didn't say it out loud. She was terrified how quickly she'd let him back in.

"Jeena," he whispered.

"I know that you can't make a commitment to me and I have to leave again." And even though she knew she shouldn't, she just wanted this one night with him. This one last night to lay the ghosts to rest. To have the closure she needed, so that she could return to Canada and know that her life here was over. And there would be no pull, nothing to lure her back.

"I want you, Maazin. Please."

He pulled her into his arms and kissed her, very intensely.

His touch felt so good. She'd forgotten how wonderful it felt to be wrapped up in Maazin's strong arms. How safe he made her feel. How he made her body sing with pleasure. When she was with him everything else melted away. There was only the two of them.

Jeena wanted to forget all the pain, the loneliness, the anger she'd felt these last ten years. For once she wanted to feel like her old self again. She wanted to feel like that girl who had been swept off her feet by her Prince Charming.

She wanted to taste passion again. Hot, heady, sweet passion.

She wanted Maazin. He was all she'd ever wanted and if she couldn't have him forever then she wanted this one night.

Jeena melted into that kiss, pressing her body against him.

"Jeena," Maazin whispered huskily. "Are you certain?"

"Yes." She ran her hands down his chest, feeling his heart beating under her palm. It was racing, just like hers. "Please just be with me. Be with me tonight for one last time."

Maazin gave in with a moan and took her in his arms, scooping her up as he'd done ten years ago on Patang Island. He carried her from the balcony into the room toward the bed.

Jeena's pulse was racing with anticipation over what was going to happen. She had missed this. She'd missed this intimacy, this connection that she had with him.

They sank onto the mattress together, kissing. His hands were in her hair. She wanted to just feel him pressed against her.

No words were needed because she knew that at this moment they both wanted the same thing.

Each other.

The kiss ended only so they could both undress each other, slowly, kissing in between because Jeena didn't want to break the connection between them. She didn't want to miss any stolen moment together.

"Jeena, I wanted you the moment I met you," Maazin whispered against her ear. "I still want you."

"I wanted you too." She was terrified of opening herself up to him. To be vulnerable to him again.

It was different this time, though.

Are you certain of that?

Jeena shook that thought from her head and let herself melt into the moment.

She wanted this.

They lay next to each other, both exposed and naked. She couldn't get enough of touching him, feeling his muscles ripple under her fingertips, running her hands over his skin and through his hair, but the most heady feeling was having his strong hands on her again.

Caressing her and making her body heat like it had been touched by electricity.

Maazin kissed her again, his lips urgent as he pulled her body flush with his.

This was it.

This was the moment. He pressed her against the mattress. His hands entwined with hers, his body so large over her she felt safe wrapped up in his arms.

Maazin gave her a kiss that seared her very soul. The warmth spread through her veins and then his lips moved from her mouth down her neck, following the erratic pulse points under her skin.

She let out a mewl of pleasure.

She wanted him inside her. Badly.

He stroked her cheek and kissed her gently again, his lips nipped softly at hers, one hand on her breast and the other stroking her between her legs. Desire coursed through her. It was overwhelming to let herself go with him.

Letting these wild emotions that she'd bottled up for so long come loose again.

He kissed her deeply as he entered her.

She cried out as he slowly filled her, wanting more of him.

She couldn't get enough of him.

She wrapped her legs around him, urging him to go even deeper, to take all of her. To completely possess her.

Everything else, all her worries, her pain, her heartache melted away in that moment that the two of them connected again. It felt so right to be with him, yet it was wrong, but she didn't care right now.

It was just the two of them moving together in complete bliss.

It wasn't long before both of them came, close together in shared pleasure. A tear slid down her cheek as it ended.

Maazin wiped it away. "Did I hurt you?"

"No, no it's just… I don't want it to end."

He kissed her. "Neither do I."

He held her close and when he rolled over on his back, he brought her against him. His arm around her, holding her tight as if he was afraid to let her go. Jeena didn't mind. She clung to him just as tightly and she was just as terrified that he would let her go as well.

It frightened her that he still had this hold on her.

The Prince she could never have.

* * *

Beautiful.

She was so beautiful. Maazin couldn't believe that it had happened again. He couldn't believe that he was here, lying in Jeena's arms again. It was what he'd dreamed about time and time again, but had never thought would be a reality.

And he was so glad that it had happened, but he was worried about what this meant.

He wasn't sure that Jeena even wanted him in her life.

Or would want him to live in Canada. If he gave up his place in the line of succession he was pretty sure it would kill his father. And then he couldn't help his people.

Also, the winter and the cold did not sound appealing in the least bit.

It would be worth it to be with her, wouldn't it?

It would be, but he couldn't leave Kalyana. He couldn't do that to his father, his mother or his brother. He'd promised Sara too that he would help with her education plans.

And why did he deserve happiness? He didn't.

Yes, you do.

And he wasn't even sure that Jeena wanted

him. She'd wanted him this night, but she'd told him it was just for this one night.

He was torn.

Maazin slowly moved and got out of the bed. He pulled on his trousers and headed out on the balcony to enjoy the night breeze. The sky was clear and full of stars. He could see the distant glow of Huban and the palace all lit up.

Usually, he didn't mind looking at Huban lit up at night, but tonight he resented that he had been born to this life. He felt so trapped.

And he was selfish for thinking that way. Ali had never thought that way. Ali had been such a good brother and good son to their parents. He would've made a great king, but they would never know that now, thanks to him.

When will you stop blaming yourself for that?

Maazin turned his back on the palace and looked at Jeena, sleeping so soundly in the bed. There had been times in the ten years they'd been apart and his heart had been broken over losing her that he'd wished that he'd never met her. And he had no doubt that she'd felt the same way too.

But now he was glad that she did. Even if

he couldn't have her forever, he was glad to be with her here at this moment.

He checked his phone and there were a few messages from Farhan.

Father is stable. Where are you? Where is Dr. Harrak?

Maazin didn't even bother responding. He'd told the security guards that he was taking a Jeep and going out to the plantation and that was all anyone needed to know. He was glad his father was stable, and that he was asking about the doctor who had performed the surgery.

All very good signs. Unless…unless his father found out he was romantically involved with Jeena and he was worried that Maazin would blow the secrecy about his engagement to Meleena being over. Perhaps Farhan had told their father about Syman.

If Jeena learned that his father knew about Syman she might flee again, and then he would never know his son.

Do you want to know him? Does he want to know you?

He knew deep down that his people would love Jeena, just as they loved Sara. And they'd be thrilled about Syman.

It was all just a dream, though. A fantasy he couldn't have, that he was afraid to have.

The sound of a phone vibrating on silent caught his attention and he noticed that Jeena had dropped her purse on the balcony floor. He picked it up and found her phone. When he touched it, it unlocked and a little boy's face looked up at him.

Oh, God. What have I done?

"You're not my mom," Syman said, confused.

"No. I'm not. Your mother is sleeping and… I heard her phone ringing."

The boy cocked his head to look at him better. "Who are you?"

"I am…" Maazin trailed off. He wanted to tell Syman that he was his father, but he couldn't. It wasn't his place. "I am Prince Maazin of Kalyana and you must be Jeena's son, Syman."

"Wow. A real prince? For real?"

"Yes," Maazin said, smiling. "Your mother has been helping out in her home country."

"I know."

Maazin could not stop staring at the boy. He saw himself in that face, but there were pieces of Ali and Farhan too.

"Well, I just wanted to speak to Mom, but if she's sleeping…" Syman trailed off as someone in the background called him. "Just talking to a prince, Grandpa. It's okay. Mom is sleeping."

There was some rushed talking in the background and Syman looked confused.

"Oh, Prince Maazin, my grandpa wants to talk to you, is that okay?"

Maazin's heart skipped a beat. "Very much okay. I will tell your mother you called."

"Okay. Here's my grandpa."

Syman's face was replaced by Mr. Harrak's and he was stunned to see Maazin.

"Your Highness," he said sternly. "Where is my daughter?"

"Sleeping. She worked very hard today on my father. The King."

Mr. Harrak's eyes widened. "What?"

"My father almost died today, Mr. Harrak, and your daughter performed a medical procedure on him at the palace. She's tired."

"She should not have been at the palace," he said worriedly. "I am sure you know why."

"I do now and I aim to find out what truly happened."

Mr. Harrak didn't look convinced. "My daughter has a tender heart. Please, Your Highness. Don't hurt her again."

"I don't want to do that, Mr. Harrak."

"We all know you are to marry Lady Meleena."

Maazin sighed. "I will not hurt her and I want to show you something." He turned the phone around. "Do you see it?"

"It's pretty dark…" Mr. Harrak said. "Is that vanilla? Is that…?"

"It's your plantation." Maazin turned the phone back again. "I own it and I will return it to your family."

"You don't need to do that, Your Highness."

"I think I do."

Mr. Harrak said nothing at first. "Thank you."

"Goodbye, Mr. Harrak."

"Your Highness."

Maazin ended the call and hadn't realized how much he'd been shaking. How sweaty his palms had become and how he'd crossed a line he hadn't intended to.

"Who were you talking to?"

Maazin spun around and saw that Jeena had got dressed again and was standing in the balcony doorway, her arms crossed, and she didn't look too pleased.

"Your father." Maazin held out the phone. Jeena took it from him. "You weren't talking only to my father. You were talking to Syman. This is his number. You were talking to our son? Why did you answer my phone? You had no right to do that."

"He's my son too," Maazin stated. "I went to get the phone to hand it to you, it unlocked and I accidentally answered it. I did not tell Syman that I am his father. Though I think he should know."

"He should, but are you going to be there for him?"

It was a valid question and he was stunned. Also, he was afraid. He didn't know the answer, he didn't have an answer for her.

Jeena looked unconvinced and she went through her messages. She frowned. "My flight home leaves in six hours."

"Six hours?" Maazin asked, his heart sinking. "I thought you had a few more days."

"The flight was bumped up. No doubt your father has regained his full faculties."

"Why do you think my father had a hand in this?" Maazin asked, confused.

"He knows about Syman! He knows about my son."

"Our son," Maazin corrected her.

Her eyes narrowed. "Would you want to keep around the former lover who bore your playboy son's illegitimate child? No, you'd ship her off so she didn't further endanger the reputation of the monarchy. You'd send her away and not have the scandal. Especially when the world thinks that son is still engaged to another woman!"

"You make my father sound like a despot. He's not. A bit of a stickler for tradition, but not a despot." It was a bad attempt at trying to lighten the mood and it only annoyed her further.

"Don't make light of this."

"I'm not. I'm telling you he had nothing to do with your orders being rescinded."

"Okay. Fine, but I'm still a threat to this secret." Jeena sighed, she shook her head. "I have to get back to my team. We have to pack to leave. You need to take me back to Huban."

"Jeena, we need to talk about this."

"What is there to talk about? I'm endangering the secret. I have to leave."

Maazin was stunned. "What're you talking about? I still don't understand how he'd know you or Syman. I didn't tell him."

"He knew me."

"He'd had sedation. People handle sedation in a very peculiar manner."

She shook her head. "He said my name

and asked about my son that plays ice hockey. He knows about my son. How?"

"That I don't know."

Jeena sighed. "It's for the best I leave."

"Are you sure?" he asked.

"Can you promise me anything?"

"You said we didn't need to promise each other anything."

"Why do you push everyone away?"

"You're doing the same thing," he snapped.

"I'm protecting my son."

"Our son."

Jeena sighed sadly. "You think you don't deserve happiness, but you do."

"I don't! It's my fault Ali is dead. I don't deserve happiness. My family can't bear to be around me. They look at me and are reminded of it all. I'm the shame of the royal family. I have to do what they want, I took away too much."

"You didn't. You say you have to do what they say, but you don't always."

"What do you mean?"

"You became a doctor, you joined the royal guard. You're freer than you think."

"How would you know? You weren't here and you're the reason why I became reckless. Losing you destroyed me!"

"And you don't think it hurt me?" she asked, her voice trembling.

"No one died because of you. I killed my brother and his wife. You were free. You had a family who loved you. I have no one."

A tear slid down her cheek. "That's right. You have no one. Take me back to my team in Huban, Maazin."

He nodded. "Of course."

There was no point in arguing any further about this. She had her orders and she had to obey them.

She had a duty to her new country, just as he had a duty to Kalyana.

They collected up their things in silent tension. There was no convincing Jeena to understand his point, and she had to leave Kalyana anyway. She had to go back to Canada and he was going to get to the bottom of this. He found it very odd that his father knew who she was and that he knew about Syman.

As they headed outside there was a flash of light, several flashes that blinded him, and Jeena screamed as Maazin realized that it was paparazzi.

She turned towards him and he held her

close, shielding her from the photographers. He didn't know how they had found them here.

Maazin got Jeena safely into the Jeep and pulled away as their vehicle was swarmed by photographers.

He sped away, leaving them far behind in the dust.

"What the heck was that?" Jeena asked, breathlessly.

"The popular press and the tabloids," he said in an undertone.

"How did they find us?"

"I don't know, but I do know one thing. If this reaches Canada, everyone will know that Syman is my son."

"This is why I shouldn't have come. This is why I should've just kept my distance from you and not told you about Syman! This is not what I want for him."

"You think I want this for him?" Maazin asked. "I don't want this life for him, but sometimes we have no choice."

"Yes. I understand that too well." Her voice shook and she didn't say more. He didn't know what to say to make it right either.

You know what to say.

He drove up to the Canadian consulate and thankfully there was no paparazzi there.

Jeena looked at him. "Please don't come to see me off tomorrow."

"Why?"

"This is going to spread everywhere and I just want to leave without drawing attention to my team. Or at least any more attention than is already being drawn. I want to leave Kalyana with my head held high."

"You can come back to Kalyana. I promised to give your father his plantation back."

"Come back to Kalyana and do what, Maazin? Have my son marked as an illegitimate son of a prince? Have the press hound me and Syman?"

"Jeena, please. I need you."

"You don't need me and you can't have my heart. Not until you stop blaming yourself for your brother's death. Not until you realize that it's your life to live. You may be a prince, but Kalyana doesn't own you as much as you think it does."

"I'm a prince. Of course Kalyana owns me and I owe my country everything," he snapped. "You don't understand what I give up for this country."

"You're right I don't fully understand, but I do understand what you're giving up. I won't put my heart in jeopardy. I did once before and it nearly destroyed me. I'm not the same person I was all those years ago."

"Jeena—"

"No. No. Goodbye, Maazin."

She slipped out of the Jeep and up the steps of the Canadian consulate, leaving him heartbroken.

Alone.

She was right. Even if her family got back their plantation there was nothing really here for her or for Syman except shame and pain. Even though Jeena hadn't broken up the engagement the world would soon think she did.

He wouldn't be able to have Syman in his life.

Unless you tell your father you're done.

And that was what Maazin was going to do. He was going to drive back to the palace and tell his father. He wanted Jeena and it didn't matter if that meant his own banishment. He wanted his son and a family with Jeena. Only Jeena. Like he always had.

He wanted her by his side. Always and forever.

CHAPTER TEN

"THIS IS OUTRAGEOUS!"

Maazin could hear his father raging from the other side of his bedchamber door. And he knew exactly what it was about. He knew that the press and the photographs of he and Jeena had come out.

Maazin knew this because he'd seen the headlines himself.

Seen the pictures of he and Jeena on the balcony, kissing and embracing. There were also photos that he hadn't been aware they'd taken, their stolen moment on Patang and when she'd stayed over at his place when they'd suspected they might have contracted dysentery.

Maazin didn't even knock when he opened the door to see his father propped up in bed and holding one of the trashy tabloid magazines in his hand.

"Father, you really shouldn't be over-exerting yourself."

His father dropped the magazine and glared at him. "What is the meaning of this?"

Maazin approached the bed and glanced at the magazine. It wasn't the only one that carried the story. Maazin and Jeena's faces had been plastered all over the national papers as well.

The headline was something along the lines of him betraying Lady Meleena. Still, they'd promised Lady Meleena that they wouldn't announce that the engagement was off for another month.

He'd broken that promise, but he was tired of taking on other people's problems. He was tired of keeping all these ridiculous secrets to avoid scandal. He was tired of blaming himself and of doing what made others happy.

Jeena was right, he had to stop blaming himself for Ali's death. He'd been so consumed these last ten years over losing her and then Ali dying that he was living in this perpetual hell of his own making.

He had to live his own life.

Ali was not coming back.

"I think you understand the meaning,

Father," Maazin said calmly. "I'm sorry that the world knows I'm not marrying Lady Meleena before everything could be smoothed over."

His father waved his hand dismissively. "I don't care. That was her father's request. So we lose some trade deals. I have more important things to worry about. What I don't want is you returning to your old foolish ways."

"What foolish ways?"

"Sleeping around. Not taking care of yourself."

Maazin smiled. "I'm not, Father."

"Aren't you?" His father pointed to the photo in the tabloid. "This is my surgeon! The Canadian surgeon, yes?"

Maazin nodded. "I love Jeena Harrak. And I have for some time."

"What do you mean, you love Dr. Harrak?" Uttam asked, confused. "You've only just met her."

"Father, don't be obtuse. You know exactly who Jeena is."

His father frowned. "I know that she was the Kalyanese Canadian who performed my procedure and that she had a son who likes hockey."

"How do you know about her son?" Maazin asked curiously.

His father waved his hand in annoyance. "I always ask for the dossiers on my physicians. It's part of their security clearance. I was intrigued by the notion of ice hockey and I was pleased that someone from Kalyana had returned to help. I was making polite conversation."

"Father, do you know why Jeena Harrak left Kalyana."

"No."

Maazin scrubbed a hand over his face. "Jeena and I were involved in a romantic attachment ten years ago, before Ali died."

Uttam looked completely lost. "What?"

"She is the daughter of a vanilla plantation owner and we were in a romantic relationship for months. Then she left and I never knew why, until she came back to Kalyana. She left because she was pregnant with my child and believed Lady Meleena when Meleena told her I didn't want her, that we'd take away her child as he or she would be illegitimate."

"She had your child?" Uttam asked, shocked.

"Yes. I have a son. My son the ice hockey player!"

Uttam leaned back against the pillows, shaking his head in disbelief. "I have a grandchild? I would never have forced Meleena on you had I known Jeena was pregnant or that you were with Jeena. I would have allowed you to marry."

Maazin nodded. "That is good to know, Father, but too little too late. Her parents sold the plantation and took her to Canada, where she gave birth to my son, Syman. My son, who I didn't get to know. My son, the ice hockey player."

"I can't believe you have a son," Uttam said quietly.

"I do. One who was stolen from me because of Meleena's meddling. Do you ever wonder why I started drinking so heavily during that time? It was because Jeena had left me and I had no idea why. Maybe if she hadn't left we'd be together and I wouldn't be blaming myself for Ali's death. Maybe Mother wouldn't hate me so much for killing her favorite son!"

Maazin heard a gasp and turned to see his mother standing behind him. He had no doubt that she'd heard every word he'd said, but he didn't care. It was the truth.

It's how he felt.

It's how she'd made him feel for the last

ten years and he was tired of letting her make him feel this way.

Maazin turned on his heel and left his father mulling all that over.

Right now he had to get to the airport and stop Jeena from getting on that flight to Canada. He had to tell her that he chose her and that he'd finally stood up for her. That he wasn't going to abandon her again. That he wanted her.

Farhan was pacing in the entranceway when Maazin came down the stairs.

"What was going on up there?" Farhan asked. "I heard all this loud talking and thought it best not to go in."

"It was for the best," Maazin said quickly. "I told Father about Jeena. And I also told him about Syman, my son with Dr. Harrak."

Farhan's eyes widened. "Wow. I'm sure he took that well."

"Well, it certainly shocked him. I have to get to the airport. I have to stop her and tell her how I feel. I can't let her out of my life again."

"And if she doesn't want this life, this life of protocol?"

Maazin sighed. "I'll give it up for her. I'll live in Canada. I'll just disappear like Bhaskar did."

Farhan groaned. "That won't help anyone."

"I know and least of all you. I never told you that I'm sorry that you're in this position. That it was my fault you are now next in line to the throne."

Farhan took his arm. "I don't blame you. Even though you've been blaming yourself for ten years, I don't blame you for what happened to Ali. He made the choice to go and get you. It was a terrible accident. You have to stop blaming yourself for his death. You have to live your life."

Maazin clapped his brother on the back. "This is what I'm trying to do. I have to stop her from going back to Canada."

"You're too late," Farhan said. "I just saw the flight off. She was on it."

Maazin's heart sunk. "Well, then I need to clear this whole thing up and then I'm going to Canada to get her back."

Jeena knew that her team had seen the tabloids and the newspapers. They were friendly enough with her, but they were keeping their distance on the long flight home and that was fine by her. Even though Maazin and Meleena's engagement had ended some time ago, the world didn't know that.

In the world's eyes she was the other woman.

She was nursing her heart, which had been wounded again.

When she'd gone back to Kalyana, the last thing she'd wanted to do had been to let her heart be hurt again by Maazin, but of course that's exactly what she'd done.

She'd been a fool and the worst part of her being humiliated was that the press had caught wind of it all and it was everywhere.

When she'd talked to her father when they'd landed in Abu Dhabi to refuel, she'd found out that the press had located her parents' place and that they had been photographing Syman. Now Syman was afraid and confused.

He didn't know what was going on.

Her heart didn't matter, but Syman's heart did. This was not what she wanted for him. Her parents were disappointed and she was disappointed in herself too.

She craned her neck and could see Calgary airport coming into view. Her stomach clenched and she hoped that there wouldn't be any press there, but she didn't have high hopes of that. They would be around.

She just hoped her father wasn't being followed or harassed.

The plane landed and she closed her eyes, hoping and praying that she could just get home and be with her son.

Jeena hurried to get off the plane. She could see that there were people staring at her as she made her way across the airport and she could see from the corners of her eyes that her face was plastered everywhere.

Oh, God.

She went to the baggage claim and tried to ignore all the pointed stares. She picked up her gear bag and then spotted her father.

He gave her a sad, worried half-smile and then took one of her bags as he leaned over and kissed her.

"Father," she whispered. "I'm so sorry."

"None of that. Let's get out of here. There is press waiting so your mother is doing circuits and is coming up again to pick us up."

"And what about Syman?"

"He's staying with his friend Thomas for the night. Thomas's mother will bring him back tomorrow morning. Early, to avoid anyone seeing him."

Jeena's stomach did a flip-flop and she tried not to be sick. She hated this.

She followed her father out into the bitter cold. Jeena kept her head down as photographers snapped pictures and she realized that this was the first time she'd had to keep her head lowered in her new country.

For the first time since she'd come to Canada this was the first time she couldn't hold her head up high and she hated that. She was the other woman here too.

She climbed into the car and tried to hold back the tears that were threatening to spill. This was the worst.

Her mother drove away and for a few moments they didn't say anything.

"Tell us what happened, Jeena," her mother said. "The press is saying a lot of things, but I want to hear it from you."

Her parents exchanged a worried look in the rearview mirror as Jeena tried to explain what had happened between Maazin and herself, and how Lady Meleena had lied to them all.

"You are in love with him," her mother said. "It's understandable. The heart is forgiving when it's in love."

Jeena nodded. "I didn't want to forgive him. I didn't want anything to do with him, but we kept getting thrown together and it happened. The King knows about Syman."

"I had no doubt that he did," her father remarked. "Especially after the Bhaskar disappearances years before. The King keeps tabs on things. At least with Princess Sara that Bhaskar mystery was solved. It was a worry in Kalyana for so long and it did, eventually, have a happy ending."

"Well, I won't be going back to Kalyana. Maazin made it very clear that duty comes before the heart."

What she didn't say was that Maazin blamed himself. He thought he didn't deserve anything. Maybe he didn't want it and he was using his guilt as an excuse.

She didn't know and she didn't care. She was tired of caring.

Her father nodded but didn't say anything, and that was for the best. She was exhausted, both physically and emotionally. She'd thought she'd found her Prince Charming, but she hadn't. There was no happy ending for her after all.

There was no prince waiting to sweep her off her feet.

There was nothing but a heart that had healed and been broken all over again, and she had no one to blame but herself for that.

All she wanted was to see her son, but she was glad he was safe with Thomas's family.

That gave her some time to figure out what she was going to tell him about his father, the Prince.

CHAPTER ELEVEN

"WHAT DO YOU MEAN, you told everyone your engagement to Lady Meleena has been off for some time?"

Maazin winced as he heard his mother snap that across the room.

"It's simple, Mother. I told you that it's time to come clean so Jeena's name can be cleared. She's not the reason the engagement ended."

Queen Aruna took a deep breath. "I do understand that, but do you realize the embarrassment that you've caused us? They think you've gone back to your playboy ways! We paid off a lot of people when Ali—"

"I know, to cover up my indiscretions."

"No!" Uttam said. "To protect you from those papers. To protect Ali and Chandni's memories, but now they're saying all these awful things about you, Maazin."

"Yes. I've seen the tabloids."

His mother frowned. "The world should know it was Meleena who had the affairs. It was Meleena who drove off Jeena. All these years. We were all fooled."

Maazin was stunned. "Sorry, what did you say? Are you saying that you're angry with me because I did throw Meleena under the bus, as it were?"

His mother sighed. "I believed Meleena when she told me Jeena wasn't really pregnant by you."

"Wait, you knew she was pregnant?"

Queen Aruna nodded. "I did, but Meleena convinced me it was a hoax. Meleena told me that Jeena was going to blackmail us. You already had a bad reputation, so I was grateful to Meleena, and she said she would help take care of the problem. She would take care of the rumor…another one of your indiscretions. I thought Meleena was doing right by you in getting Jeena to leave, by paying her off and sticking by you."

"I still don't understand. How did you know Jeena was pregnant?"

"The doctor informed me. I knew you were in love with Jeena. I was happy, but then Meleena convinced me it was a lie and that Jeena was using you. I wanted to protect you."

"Meleena hurt us all," Maazin said bitterly.

"She may not have loved you but she wanted to marry you, Maazin, so she lied to all of us."

"I remember," Maazin said. "Now I remember that."

Uttam nodded. "She found out about Dr. Harrak's pregnancy and took it on herself to ruin your life. Meleena knew that you were going to choose Jeena and not her."

Seeing his son's furious expression, he reached out and placed his hand on Maazin's arm. "She's gone, Maazin. She's not worth your time. She's someone else's problem now."

"That's not good enough! She cost me ten years with the woman I love. She cost me time with my son!"

"I am sorry." Aruna motioned for Maazin to sit on the edge of the bed, where she was sitting next to Uttam. It looked like his mother was about to cry. "No one should lose precious time with their child. I have wasted time with you, Maazin. I was scared your reckless lifestyle would cost me you as well, but I want you to know I don't blame you for Ali's death."

"You don't?" Maazin asked, stunned.

"No. I thank God every day you survived. Oh, at first I was angry that you had gone and done something foolish. That you were reckless again, but Ali did not have to go and get you, and it was an accident."

"That's what Farhan said," Maazin said quietly.

Uttam nodded. "He will make a fine king. One day. Not soon!"

Aruna smiled. "Stop blaming yourself, Maazin. You deserve to be happy. Ali would want that."

Maazin took his mother's hands. "And he would want you to be happy too."

Aruna's smile wobbled. "I will try. I am sorry if you've blamed yourself all this time. I don't blame you. I love you."

Maazin hugged his mother while she cried, and he felt a huge weight lift from his shoulders.

Maazin smiled at his parents. "So what do I do?"

"You go and you marry Dr. Harrak. You marry her and make things right. You may have lost those years with your son, but he's still young and you have time with him. Cherish that time with him and bring him to Kalyana." Uttam's chest puffed out. "Illegitimate or not, he is my grandson and I want him here with me. Life is too short."

"What do you think, Mother?"

Aruna brushed away a tear. "I want to know my grandson too. I want to know Syman and I want to apologize to Jeena. It's my fault as well. I am sorry my grief over the loss of Ali has made you feel that way, but when Uttam told me we have a grandchild, well…" More tears gathered in her eyes. "I want to meet him."

"I do too." Maazin stood up and kissed his mother on the cheek. "I'll have to take the private jet, then, to Canada. And we'll have to call the prime minster and get clearance to enter Canada."

"You leave that to me," Uttam said, and then he saw the stern look from his wife, which basically told him that he was treading on dangerous ground. "Or perhaps Farhan can arrange it?"

"Thank you, Father." Maazin bowed quickly and turned to leave.

"Maazin, wait!" his mother called out.

Maazin turned around and his mother held out a ring. "It was Queen Narubi's ring. Please give it to Dr. Harrak. Please let her know that we welcome her here. Explain to her it was not our doing. We were led to believe the wrong thing. Had we known the truth…she wouldn't have had to leave. She is welcome here and she would make a good wife for you. I'm sorry."

"That's right," Uttam shouted from the bed. "If I'd known that you were in love with her and that she was pregnant with our grandchild, I would've insisted you marry her straight away."

"Thank you." Maazin kissed his mother on the cheek again. "I will make this right. I promise."

And if Jeena didn't want to marry him and come to Kalyana, he would let her be, but he was hoping that in her heart she still loved him, just as much as he loved her.

He wanted her to know that she would be safe and protected. That she wouldn't be trapped. Things were changing and they were changing for the better. Perhaps this was a life he would want for his son.

Perhaps it wasn't so bad after all.

Maybe together he and Farhan could change the face of the Kalyanese monarchy.

And if Jeena did agree to come and be his wife, he would have to go about building some kind of indoor ice rink so that his son could keep up with hockey. Just the thought of that brought a smile to his face.

The whole future lay ahead, bright and full of sunshine.

If only Jeena would say yes.

Farhan had worked with the Canadian government to make sure that no one got wind of Maazin's arrival in Calgary. He didn't want Jeena to know that he was coming. Or the media. He didn't want her to flee.

He wanted to let her know that she would've been accepted.

One petty person whose pride had been hurt had ruined their lives for the last ten years and Maazin only hoped that it wasn't too late. He only hoped that he hadn't ruined his chance with her.

Kavan, Farhan's bodyguard, had accompanied Maazin to Canada and was going to make sure that the press kept their distance, as well as drive him to Jeena's home. Farhan had insisted on it because Kavan had been with him when he'd gone to Canada to track down Sara, and he was familiar with the country and driving conditions there in snowy and icy conditions.

As the plane approached the runway at Calgary International Airport Maazin let out a shudder when he saw white on the ground. In the distance he could see the city and smoke rising from the buildings into the clear blue sky.

The large Calgary Tower stuck out in the skyline.

"It's very cold down there, Your Highness," Kavan commented.

"I agree," Maazin said. "Jeena told me it was cold."

"I think this is colder than those ski trips that you and your brothers took in Kitzbühel."

"I believe you're right." Maazin shuddered. "You made sure that customs has already cleared us and that the Canadian government is on board with our hushed operation?"

"I have the assurances from the prime minister himself. He's quite a charismatic man."

Maazin smiled. "I'm glad to hear he's so accommodating."

The plane landed smoothly and was directed to a private runway on the far side of the airport, reserved for foreign dignitaries, royalty and the prime minister.

There was a small fleet of cars waiting, which would accommodate Maazin's small

staff and security. As requested, the Kalyanese consulate hadn't added the flags to
the cars as it was a private visit and Maazin
didn't want to catch any one's attention as
they made their way north out of Calgary to
a small ranch between Calgary and Airdrie.

It would be easy to locate the Harraks'
ranch, because it was the only property
in the vicinity that had a large number of
greenhouses, and the Harraks were known
for growing and selling poinsettias.

As Maazin stepped off the plane it felt
like his skin was being cut by sharp knives.
It was bitterly cold and he didn't like it one
bit, but for Jeena he would brave anything.
Even freezing cold temperatures and biting,
nasty wind.

The Kalyanese ambassador to Canada
was waiting and he was wearing a parka.

"Your Highness, I have a parka for you."

Maazin nodded and gladly allowed the
ambassador to slip it on his shoulders. "This
is awful!"

"Nothing like beautiful Kalyana weather."
The ambassador smiled. "Everything is
ready for all your people."

"Thank you."

The ambassador stepped back, the door to
the SUV with tinted windows was opened

and he slipped inside. Kavan took his place in the driver's seat. Maazin adjusted the temperature settings in the back and then slipped off the parka.

"Are you ready, Your Highness?" Kavan asked from the front.

"Yes. Let's go." Maazin touched the breast pocket of his designer suit to make sure Queen Narubi's ring was still there. His pulse was racing as Kavan punched in the co-ordinates on the GPS and then slowly drove away from the private jet. The rest of Maazin's people were going to the embassy in Calgary.

There would be a car following them for security, at his father's insistence. If Maazin had his way, he wouldn't, but then again, with the media pestering Jeena and her family and his son, he didn't want to take any chances.

He sat back and looked out at the scenery, which was very different from Kalyana's. They drove north on a large highway with cars everywhere. He noticed a lot of the vehicles on the highway were trucks and they were all white.

"Why do you suppose so many of the vehicles are white, Kavan?"

"Something to do with the oil fields, Your Highness, but I'm not certain."

"Oil fields?" Maazin really didn't know much about Canada, but one thing was for certain, the endless stretch of open plains without trees or sea to break the horizon was slightly unsettling. But if this was where Jeena was happy, if this was where she wanted Syman to stay, he would get used to it.

He would stay and do whatever she wanted.

He wasn't leaving without her. He wasn't walking away from her again, even though he didn't know that he had done that in the first place. He didn't know that she had been sent away. All these years he'd thought she left him.

And for all these years she'd thought he'd walked away from her.

Now it was time to make everything right.

It was time for him to claim his family, like he should've done ten years ago.

It felt like it took an eternity to drive forty minutes to the outskirts of Calgary and then on a side road off the highway that turned into a gravel road that had a sign pointing to the Harraks' greenhouses.

Maazin couldn't believe the large stretch of land that Mr. Harrak possessed. It put his small vanilla plantation to shame. Before they even reached the main house Maazin could see the greenhouses and through the fogged windows he could see the red of the poinsettias.

Kavan made another turn and they approached a raised ranch-style house. Kavan drove as close as he could. Maazin's pulse was thundering in his ears. To the side of the ranch house there was a small ice rink and there were kids out on it now, skating. He couldn't help but wonder which of those boys was Syman.

He was finally going to meet his son.

"Hey, Mom! There's a strange car parked in front of the house!" Syman shouted as he skated by her, gesturing wildly.

Oh, no.

Jeena turned around and was worried that the press was ignoring her father's restraining order and they were coming to get a glimpse of Syman again. Her phone was in the house because it was so cold out that the battery would die within minutes.

She hoped that her father had seen the cars approach and had the good sense to call the Royal Canadian Mounted Police about the restraining order violation. The RCMP had promised to protect her after a particularly intrepid paparazzo had gotten into one of the greenhouses and done substantial damage as he'd tried to get information about her parents.

Not to mention one photographer who had scared Syman senseless when he'd got off the school bus.

Since she'd got back three days ago there had been endless harassment.

And she was getting sick and tired of it.

She started marching in the direction of the SUV when she saw who had got out of the back. She froze in her tracks and her heart skipped a beat.

Maazin?

He was completely inappropriately dressed for this crazy cold snap that they were currently having.

"Maazin?" she called out.

He spun around and then started walking toward her.

"Jeena, thank goodness…"

"What're you doing?"

"I've come to see you."

"I get that. I mean, you're going to freeze to death standing out here without a coat on." She glanced behind her. "Why don't you have a coat?"

"I do. I left it in the car."

"Let's get inside and tell Kavan to come in as well. It's too cold to leave the car running."

"Well, if it's too cold, why are there children out there, playing on the ice?" Maazin asked.

"They're dressed for it and they'll be heading inside soon. They had to get their practice in. My father can manage the boys. He'll take them into the greenhouse staff lunch room for hot chocolate. Let's go into the main house."

Maazin nodded and motioned to Kavan, who was shivering as well.

Jeena opened the door and ushered them both inside.

"Mother!" Jeena called out. "We have guests."

"Oh, no. Not the press again!" Her mother came around the corner and then froze in her tracks when she saw Maazin. She instantly curtseyed. "Your Highness."

"Please. There is no need to do that, Mrs. Harrak."

Her mother stood up slowly and then looked at Jeena for an explanation. Jeena shrugged and took off her bulky winter gear.

"Mom, will you take Kavan into the kitchen and give him a nice hot cup of coffee?"

Her mother nodded. "Of course. Follow me, Kavan."

Kavan waited until Maazin nodded and then followed her mother into the kitchen. She finished taking off her winter gear and then stood in front of Maazin, completely shocked that he was here in Canada and standing in her parents' front hall. It was surreal. Of all the scenarios she'd pictured in her mind of Maazin coming to get her, this had not been one of them. A royal prince of Kalyana, wearing an expensive suit and standing in a tiny front hall that was littered with twenty pairs of wet snow boots, not to mention a bunch of knapsacks.

"It smells a lot like feet here," he teased, obviously trying to break the tension.

"You're standing by the shoe rack and there are a lot of sweaty boots there."

Maazin glanced down. "So I see."

"What're you doing here?" she asked, still feeling stunned.

"I came to see you."

"Why?" she asked.

"Is there a place with more privacy where we can talk?" he asked.

"Sure. Follow me." Jeena didn't want to

talk with him in the house because Syman might come bursting in after all his friends had been picked up. Attached to the house was her father's first greenhouse and it was a place where he still grew a small batch of vanilla orchids. It was quiet and warm in there.

She led him into the greenhouse and shut the door behind them.

Maazin looked around. "Your father grows vanilla here as well?"

"Just a small batch. He sells it on the weekends at a local organic market." She crossed her arms. Her heart was still hammering in her chest and she couldn't quite believe that Maazin was here, in Canada.

"So, will you finally tell me what you're doing here?" she asked.

"I came for you."

She blinked a couple of times. "Pardon me?"

"Jeena, you know I'm not marrying Lady Meleena. The moment I dropped you off at the Canadian embassy in Huban I went straight to the palace to have it out with my parents. I told them I was tired of hiding the fact I'm not marrying Meleena and I was going to marry you."

"I thought you couldn't promise me anything? I thought you didn't deserve happiness?"

"I was wrong."

She tried not to let her mouth drop open in shock. Her pulse was thundering in her ears and it was very hard to breathe. "How did your parents react to your news?"

"Not well at first."

"Of course. I'm the last person they'd want you to marry."

"No, you need to stop that. It's because my father didn't know Syman was mine. Meleena had them all believing you were going to blackmail us. They believed Meleena paid you off and saved the royal family from another one of my scandals. Meleena wanted to marry me, so she hurt us both. She lied to us both."

Jeena swallowed the hard lump that was forming her throat. "What?"

"My father wants you to know that he would never have forced me to marry Meleena had he known I wanted you. He would've been thrilled had he known you were pregnant with my child. My mother is thrilled too, but Meleena had convinced her you weren't pregnant. In fact, they're both very happy to have a grandson. They both want to meet him."

The room began to spin and Jeena didn't know how to take this information. She sat down on a bench and took a couple of deep breaths.

"I don't… I don't know what to say. We have a life here in Canada…"

"I know and if that is what you choose, then I choose it too."

"You choose it too?" she asked, confused.

Maazin dropped to his knees in front of her and took her hands in his strong ones. "You're trembling."

"I'm scared," she whispered.

"I am too, but if Canada is where you need to be then I will live here. What I can't do is live without you in my life. I can't live without Syman in my life. I've spent too many years thinking that I didn't deserve happiness or love because of my actions, but I was wrong. I was wrong about so many things. You were right, but I was scared. Scared to lose you again."

Jeena didn't know what to say. Tears stung her eyes, because he was saying all the right things. It was everything she'd wanted to hear ten years ago. It was everything she'd wanted to hear four days ago.

"How can you live in Canada? Your duty is to Kalyana. You're a prince."

"I can live wherever I want and return to Kalyana if I'm needed, but if you choose to come to Kalyana with Syman, you can continue your work there. My father has already passed the decrees and legislation to start the ball rolling on a university. A university that promotes the STEM program to women. Sara still wants your input."

"Are you serious?"

"Yes. The University of Kalyana will happen and it will happen in the next year."

"I'm glad to hear that." She was still shocked. "The world thinks I'm the other woman."

"No. My father straightened it all out and will make a formal speech soon. After the whole Bhaskar thing, the people don't want heirs running off. They don't want scandal for Kalyana. Everyone is thrilled we have a child."

"Oh." Jeena still couldn't seem to think straight. It was everything she'd wanted to hear ten years ago. She couldn't quite believe it.

Maazin reached into his pocket and pulled out a ring. One that she had seen on the hand of Queen Aruna. "Marry me, Jeena. Marry me like you were supposed to have done ten years ago."

Her pulse raced and she felt like she was going to faint.

"Yes," she whispered.

"Yes?"

She nodded. "Yes."

He slipped the ring on her finger and kissed her, and she couldn't stop the flow of tears. Tears that she had been holding back for so long they came pouring out of her. Maazin kissed away those tears and held her.

"I'm so sorry, Jeena. So sorry for it all."

"It's not your fault. I should've trusted you. I was terrified to be pregnant and alone in a country so far away from the one I knew. I blamed myself too. I blamed myself for letting you take my heart when I felt like I didn't deserve you."

"You deserve me, but I don't deserve you," Maazin said.

"Yes, you do."

They kissed again.

"And I would like to go back to Kalyana," she whispered.

"What about Syman and his life here?" Maazin asked.

"We can always come back and visit. My parents will stay here. I know that. They have found happiness here. And I wouldn't leave them behind unless I knew that there was a private jet to come and get them whenever they wanted to come home." She was teasing him.

He smiled at her. "Of course. Whenever they want to do that and whenever Syman wants to return to Canada, we will get him here. He'll just have to get used to bodyguards and security."

"Mom? Where are you?"

Jeena took a deep breath and stood up. Maazin followed her and she could tell that he was nervous.

"It'll be okay, Maazin. I've told him. He knows."

"He does?"

Jeena nodded. "It's okay. He wants to know you. You deserve to be in his life."

Maazin nodded. "Yes. Good. I want to be his father. I want him in my life."

"And he will be. It might take some time, but he wants to know you."

Syman came running into the greenhouse. "Mom, you won't believe—"

Syman stopped and stared up at Maazin. "It's you! The Prince I talked to over the phone."

"Yes. It's a pleasure to finally meet you." Maazin held out his hand and Syman shook it.

"What're you doing here?" Syman asked.

"I've come to ask your mother to marry me," Maazin said.

Syman looked at her. "Mom?"

"Syman, Prince Maazin is your father. You remember me talking about those newspaper men and other people following you around?"

"You mean that I'm a prince?"

"Yes," Maazin said. "I'm afraid so."

Syman nodded. "Cool."

Maazin knelt down to look Syman in the eyes. "I'm sorry I've been away for a long time."

"Mom said you didn't know about me."

"I didn't, and it's no one's fault, but know this, if I had known about you I would've come sooner. Do you forgive me?"

"Yes." Syman nodded. "You're here now for good?"

"I'm staying for as long as you need to, before I return to Kalyana."

Syman frowned. "Mom?"

"The thing is, we have to move to Kalyana for a while," Jeena said. "Are you okay with that?"

Syman worried his bottom lip. "Do they have hockey there?"

"No," Maazin said. "Not yet, but your grandfather the King promised that a hockey arena would be built and maybe you could show the other children there how to play."

Syman cocked his head to one side. "I like that, but what about Grandma and Grandpa? Would we ever see them again?"

"Of course, whenever we wanted," Jeena said. "And they can come back to Kalyana and see you. For now, for a little while, we have to go back to Kalyana. You have to meet your other grandparents and your uncle and his wife."

Syman nodded. "So we get to go on a plane trip?"

Maazin chuckled. "Yes. A private jet, in fact."

"Cool. Okay, I'm okay with this. Can I go ask Grandma for a cookie?"

Jeena laughed. "Sure."

"Thanks!" Syman ran off.

"That was relatively easy," Maazin remarked.

"It'll take some time for him to process it," Jeena admitted dryly. "Then there will be a lot of questions."

"It'll take some time for him to get to

know me. I understand that. I'm willing to wait." Maazin wrapped his arms around her. "I'm just not willing to wait ten years again to make you my wife."

"Neither am I. I love you, Maazin. I always have. There has never been any one else. I've only loved you. I've only ever wanted you."

Maazin tipped her chin. "I've only loved you and from that first moment that I saw you out on the polo field, you're all I've ever wanted as well. You're all I'll ever want. I was a fool to think otherwise."

Jeena laughed and kissed him gently. "Yes. Yes, you were."

Maazin ended up spending two weeks in Canada. There was a lot to do to prepare for the journey back to Kalyana.

Instead of staying at the embassy, though, he stayed at the Harraks' home, so that he could get to know Syman better. And though it took some time, Syman accepted Maazin as his father and was soon showing him the affection he so desperately wanted from his son. Affection he'd never thought he deserved.

Maazin reveled in those moments when he was able to tuck Syman in for the night and have the boy wrap his arms around him and call him Dad. That meant so much to him. The more that he got to know his son, the more of Ali and even his father he saw in him.

There was a stubborn, defiant streak in Syman that reminded Maazin very much of his father. And Ali too. And Maazin knew that deep down Syman and Uttam were like two peas in a pod.

Jeena, with the help of higher up government officials in Canada and Kalyana, was honorably discharged from her services to the Canadian armed forces. It was hard for Jeena to let go of her team, but she had plans to work closely with Sara and promote that program about women in the STEM program in the new university.

That gave her something to be passionate about and something to do beyond a life of protocol and charity events.

Maazin, Jeena, Syman and the Harraks had all watched King Uttam's speech to the media about Jeena and Syman. It was clear from the public's feedback that no one held any animosity toward Jeena. No one thought she was the other woman any more and Kalyana was excited to have another royal heir.

And although Maazin offered them their vanilla plantation back, Jeena's parents were much happier in Canada.

They hated being so far away from Jeena, but they were glad that they could return to their homeland with their heads held high and that their daughter was soon to be a princess.

Or rather she *was* a princess because before they left Canada Jeena and Maazin married in a civil ceremony at the Kalyana embassy and Syman was legitimized.

The line of succession would soon change yet again as Sara, Farhan's wife, was expecting a baby.

And that was fine by Maazin.

When they boarded the private jet at Calgary International Airport there was a lot of media waiting to get a glimpse of the new royal family of Kalyana, but Kavan and his team of security managed to keep the media at a distance.

It excited Syman that the prime minister of Canada had come out to see them off and that he was going on his first ever plane ride.

Of course, the novelty of a long flight soon wore off on Syman, but Maazin enjoyed having him on the plane and keeping him entertained by playing games with him and reading with him. Syman had a hard time sleeping but finally drifted off on the last leg of the trip from Abu Dhabi to Huban.

Maazin made sure he was secured on the couch portion of the private jet and covered him with a blanket, and he slept there for the last few hours.

"I hope we can wake him in enough time to see the welcome ceremony when we land," Jeena remarked. "I also hope he's not too grumpy for your father. He's a bit of a grumpy bear when you wake him up too soon."

Maazin smiled. "The same with my father. They're so alike."

"I hope that it goes smoothly." She was worrying her bottom lip again.

"It will. Trust me. My parents are thrilled."

"It's hard to do that. Even though I really should, because it wasn't your fault and it wasn't my fault. I'm glad that whole thing is behind us and I'm glad Meleena is no longer in Kalyana."

"Yes. She's safer away from Kalyana too, because if I ever see her again I'm going to— She's better off far away. She cost me too much." Maazin glanced back at Syman, who was rousing as the plane began to descend as they got closer to Huban.

"Well, we can't maim her we're both doctors and we've promised to do no harm." Jeena winked.

"That remains to be seen," Maazin teased.

Jeena started rubbing her hands together. She was wearing her mother's treasured sari, the one she'd managed to save, the one she'd bought on Petrie Island that the weaver, Mr. Patel, had made.

"That color suits you," Maazin said. "Your mother has good taste."

"I think so too. It's always been one of my favorites and I wanted to show my support for the people."

"Smart." Maazin took her hand and kissed it. "You will make an excellent princess."

The plane made its final descent into Huban and Jeena managed to wake Syman up. He was grumpy for a few moments, but when he realized they were landing and that soon he'd meet the rest of his family, he perked up.

The plane landed and Maazin could already hear the crowds cheering. As the plane taxied around he could see a sea of blue, green and gold flags waving and the red carpet, with the royal motorcade waiting at the end.

This was it.

The plane's engines stopped and Maazin took her hand, giving it a squeeze. Then he took Syman's hand and the door opened.

Maazin stepped out of the plane with Syman by his side. The cheers were deafening and Syman trembled.

"It's okay. They're happy you're here. Just wave."

Syman worried his bottom lip like his mother and then waved.

Jeena came behind them and they walked down the steps together. When they reached the red carpet King Uttam and Queen Aruna, followed by Farhan and Sara, came to meet them.

Maazin could see that his father was having a hard time hiding his emotions as he looked at the little boy who was so obviously his grandson.

And Uttam broke protocol to get down on one knee and hold out a Kalyanese flag to his little grandson.

"Welcome to Kalyana, Syman."

Syman smiled at him and took the flag and then did what Maazin had not expected and threw his arms around Uttam's neck.

Uttam was shocked, but then wrapped his arms around the boy and lifted him up in his arms, beaming with pride.

Jeena was fighting back tears.

Uttam turned to her. "Welcome home, Dr. Harrak. Or should I say Princess Jeena?"

"Your Majesty." Jeena curtseyed and Maazin bowed.

"Let's get out of here, shall we?" Uttam set Syman down and took his hand in his.

Maazin took Jeena's hand and both of them turned to the cheering crowds and waved.

"I'm a bit scared," Jeena whispered.

"Don't be scared. I shall protect you. I shall always protect you and I will never let anyone hurt you again. I love you."

"I love you too, Your Highness."

EPILOGUE

One year later

"Now!" BELLOWED UTTAM from across the cricket pitch. "Isn't this much better than ice hockey?"

Syman lowered the cricket bat. "No, but it's fun. I like it, Grandpapa."

Uttam laughed. "Good!"

"Good!" Sophie squawked from her outside perch, making Syman laugh, which in turn made Uttam laugh and then Aruna laughed from where she was sitting under an awning with her newest grandchild, Farhan and Sara's little boy, Ali, in her arms.

Jeena was wandering away from the cricket and the tent. She was hot and uncomfortable and still had a couple months left of her pregnancy.

Her parents were coming for a visit soon and she couldn't wait to see them again.

They video-called most nights with Syman, and Maazin had taken Syman and her back once to visit them, but once Jeena had found out she was pregnant, with twins no less, she couldn't go anywhere and she was feeling a bit cooped up.

Maazin had been busy with the university plans and helping to get Kalyana back on its feet. New homes were being built. Homes and businesses on Petrie Island, and many of the other islands, were almost all rebuilt now and things were going smoothly.

Kalyana was thriving again and would be more than ready if another cyclone like Blandine hit. Jeena loved being back in her home country, though she did miss Canada, but she loved being with her people again and being with Maazin. If only she could get back to work.

She really hated not being able to work out in the field, but Maazin was being way too overprotective.

"Where do you think you're going?"

Jeena turned around to see Maazin strolling towards her, carrying a glass of iced tea. He handed her the glass and she gladly took a sip.

"I was uncomfortable. The canopy your

mother had set up might keep the sun off everything, but it doesn't keep out the heat."

Maazin reached out and touched her belly. "You really should be sitting down. With twins you could be early. You're a doctor, you should know better."

"Haven't you ever heard that doctors make the worst patients?"

Maazin cocked an eyebrow. "No. I haven't heard that."

"Well, they do." Jeena sighed. "I promise I'll go and sit down again. I just wanted a little walk to see if I could catch a breeze."

Maazin kissed the top of her head. "Remember the cool breezes on Patang Island?"

"Yes. I do." She closed her eyes. "Are you offering to take me there?"

"No. Not in your condition, but tonight when we go home we can go for a swim in the pool. Just the two of us."

"What about Syman?"

"He wants to spend the night with Grandpapa."

They both looked back to see their son finally catch a cricket ball on the end of his bat. The ball rolled over to Uttam who fell back, acting like he'd been hit, but really was hoping to catch Syman unawares to get a hug from him.

"They really are alike, aren't they?" Jeena asked.

"It's uncanny." And it was. She had always sort of suspected that Syman's stubborn streak and athletic side came from Maazin's side of the family. She'd just had no idea how well Syman would take to Uttam. Syman also loved Farhan and Sara. And since Sara was Canadian as well, she understood what it meant when he used words like "tuque" and "pop" to her.

And Syman doted on his newest cousin. Almost like a big brother would.

Syman fit in so seamlessly with his newfound family it did her heart good.

"So, what do you think? Do you want to go for a swim later with me?" her husband asked huskily, interrupting her thoughts.

Jeena stood on tiptoe. "How about we go back now? No one will notice if we leave."

"They'll notice if we leave. Father has this big meal planned with some dignitaries and… You don't look too impressed."

"I'm exhausted and I think if we told your father that I was he'd let us leave now. Do you really feel like having a dinner with all these stuffy people and talk politics in this heat?"

Maazin wrinkled his nose. "No. You're right. Not particularly."

"I think he'll understand if we slip away." She wrapped her arms around him. "We can go home and swim now. We can also swim later and then just spend the rest of the evening in bed."

"I think that plan is what got you into this condition in the first place," Maazin teased.

Jeena laughed. "What do you say, Your Highness?"

Maazin chuckled and kissed her. "That sounds like a good plan, my love. That sounds like a good plan indeed."

"Good." She kissed him. "Have I told you today that I love you?"

"No, but why don't you tell me now?" he said archly as he kissed her again.

"I love you. I didn't believe in all those old fairy-tales, the ones where a prince came and swept a girl off her feet, but now I'm a believer."

Maazin caressed her cheek. "I just wish my sweeping you off your feet had gone a bit more smoothly and in a more timely fashion."

"That only happens in movies. Real life is a lot messier and I wouldn't have it any other way."

Maazin kissed her again before taking her hand as they walked off together.

Happy that their happily-ever-after had come at last.

* * * * *

If you missed the previous story in the Cinderellas to Royal Brides duet, look out for

Surgeon Prince, Cinderella Bride
by Ann McIntosh

And if you enjoyed this story, check out these other great reads from Amy Ruttan

The Surgeon's Convenient Husband
Carrying the Surgeon's Baby
NY Doc Under the Northern Lights
A Date with Dr. Moustakas

All available now!